PARIS AND THE REAPER

A SOUL TO FIND NOVEL

LAYLA REYNE

ABOUT THIS BOOK

I was given the name Paris at birth.
So far, I've lived up to it; or rather, down to it.
Too pretty, too unfocused, too easy a target.
My father even tried to sacrifice me.

And then I was saved by a beautiful, haunted man.

Mac is a reaper; he delivers lost souls.
But when he came for mine, I wouldn't let go.
And now I can hear other souls too.
I can help him. Love him, if he'll let me.

Assuming we survive a conspiracy to bring Chaos through
the veil.

Mac says souls get what they deserve.
If I do enough good, then maybe I can be worthy of his.
Maybe I can hold on to him and our bond—forever.

Paris and the Reaper is a soft, swoony, and suspenseful M/M urban fantasy romance. It features a grumpy raven shifter afraid to love and lose again and the sweet, cursed human who makes him want to risk it all.

For John Boy and JoJo

PART ONE

PARIS

ONE

PARIS AND PAIN were old friends.

His first memory was of pain, his lungs burning as his mouth and nose filled with water, as he struggled against the hands that held him under. That was the first time his father had tried to kill him.

Pain had accompanied every encounter with his father since.

The force of his closed fist, the sting of his open palm, the pointy tips of his loafers that pummeled him when he was down.

The sharper sting of his words that buried him deeper.

Why are you such a fool?

You're too soft.

Put away those stupid brushes.

I can't believe she gave her life for you.

The last was his father's favorite, a constant reminder of the guilt Paris lived with every day and that his father never let him forget.

They were also the last words Vincent had uttered when

he'd shoved him into the seemingly frail arms of the small, bearded man in a waist apron. Paris tried to run but barely made it two steps before the stranger had stopped him in his tracks with nothing but his glowing red eyes.

Paris had known then that this was another of Vincent's attempts to kill him. And as he lay spread eagle on a cold hard altar, his hands and feet bound, blood seeping from searing cuts along the insides of his arms and thighs, Paris thought maybe his father had finally succeeded.

Beside the altar, the once small man stood taller than any person Paris had ever seen. No, not a person. A monster—a giant—with those same glowing red eyes, but where he'd had a coarse, curly beard before, he now had a nest of writhing snakes that feasted on Paris's open wounds. As they sank their fangs into his muscles and sucked his blood, their master sucked more of his life—his soul—to feed the shimmering orbs of magic that grew bigger and brighter in the air above his hands.

He spoke in tongues Paris didn't recognize, but as his voice escalated into louder more urgent chants, the pain escalated too, the snakes biting harder. Paris's soul cried out in his ears, joined by other souls crying out too. Each new one like a knife carving up through the altar beneath him, into his skin, creating a path for the souls to burrow inside and chilling him to his core. Magnifying the pain. All those souls being ripped through him. It was torture beyond anything his father had ever inflicted on him.

I can't believe she gave her life for you.

Except that.

He opened his eyes and blinked through the pain and tears that clouded his vision. He searched for the stars above, for that place a nanny had once told him his mother had gone to the day he'd been born. Bright, shining hope was there for one brief instant, the fog breaking long enough for him to glimpse the only love he'd ever known, the love he'd finally get to meet soon, before the dense gray clouds rolled back in and took the light away.

And brought something dark with them.

Something darker even than his father's hands holding him under the water. Something that intended to take his soul and all the other souls screaming with his. Something that intended to wreak chaos on Yerba Buena and beyond.

The orbs in the monster's hands burned so bright that Paris had to squint against their blinding glare.

New voices—words he recognized—cut through the chants.

"Does anyone see him?"

"He's on the altar!"

KRAA.

Roaring, the monster hurled the relatively dimmer of the two balls of fire the direction of the voices.

And then another, different kind of darkness flew at the altar—an undulating mass of black, the fluttering of wings sending a cool breeze wafting across Paris's prone body. The flock of black birds dive-bombed the monster, plucking away his snakes one by one. Paris shouted with each painful yank of their fangs out of his skin; the giant shouted louder with each subject ripped from his body and cast aside until none were left.

Until the biggest black bird of all, a giant raven, flew talons-first at the monster's eyes.

He howled and staggered beside the altar, trying to swat the raven away with the hand not holding the magical orb, but the raven wasn't backing down. He came at the giant, again and again, while other voices shouted in the background.

"Mac, watch the globe."

"We need to neutralize it."

"Adam, take the shot!"

KRAA.

The familiar sound of gunfire rent the air and fear rocketed up Paris's spine. He didn't want the raven to be hit. But the bullet, it turned out, was the least of their worries. Before it reached the monster, the fireball in his hand exploded, engulfing him and singeing Paris's skin.

"No!" Paris shouted, his voice rough, barely a whisper, but no less urgent, no less filled with fear for the fate of his rescuer.

He scrunched closed his eyes and screamed through the pain and fear until the heat began to recede, until cool air wafted over him once more.

A gentle weight landed on his chest, and for a moment it felt like freedom, like his soul could breathe knowing the raven had lived and would carry him to the love waiting for him above.

But then another voice called to him. *Help me.*

And another, then another, more and more until the cacophony of pleas were as loud as the thunderous waves that crashed against the cliffs beneath the condo he called home.

He shook his head, trying and failing to block out the noise.

KRAA!

He opened his eyes and locked his gaze with the violet one staring down at him. The sense of freedom was gone, but in its place was a lifeline Paris's soul grabbed onto with both hands.

The raven jumped, its giant wings fluttering.

KRAA!

Paris didn't let go, even as pain ricocheted through his head and darkness clouded the edge of his vision. The riot in his ears coalesced into those same two words, over and over, the only two he could manage before his own world went dark.

"Help me."

———

Paris liked soft things.

In a world that was sharp and brutal, soft was the sensory antithesis of violence. The buttery leather of his car seats, the silky bristles of fresh paint brushes, the plush warmth of cotton jersey, the delicate threads of satin and lace.

The gentle brush of skin on skin. His best friends' arms hooked through his. A courtesan's tender touch. The backs of someone's fingers stroking his temple, oh so softly, and ruffling his hair.

He moved to tilt his head, to chase after the feather-light touch, but barely managed to angle his chin before pain lanced through him. His head, his arms, his legs were all on fire.

Fire.

Like the globes that had hovered above the monster's hands.

As the horrific, terrifying past came rushing back, so did nausea and bile, rocketing up his throat. He shifted, needing to sit up before he choked on the sick, but fucking hell, the pain.

Far beyond anything his father had ever inflicted on him.

But his father had done this, hadn't he? Had offered him as some kind of sacrifice. Had almost succeeded in killing him this time.

"Fuck," he cursed, and even that hurt.

"I've got you," someone said, their voice deep and calm, soft in its own way. Like their fingers had been. "Let's get you on your side."

Gritting his teeth, Paris let the person help roll him. Just in time, the pain and his roiling stomach conspiring to expel what little was in it. He couldn't remember the last time he'd eaten. Couldn't fathom it now, the thought of food sending another wave of bile up and out and into a bucket.

Shuddering, he struggled for breath, for some relief from the anvils in his head and the needles in his limbs.

"You get it all out?" the voice asked.

He nodded weakly and—sweet mercy—was rolled onto his back again. A wet cloth was swiped over his lips then laid across his forehead, and with the soft, cool dampness came the needed respite, enough for him to breathe, to open his eyes and look up into the dark ones above him. Gone were the violet eyes, gone were the black feathers and hooked beak, gone were the talons that had scratched out the monster's eyes. But Paris was certain the man above him, with his tan skin, sharp nose, and black hair was the same as the raven who'd saved him.

"It hurts," he told the stranger.

"Where?"

Paris chuckled at the inane question, then winced when the motion brought more daggers, in his head worst of all.

"Hold on," the raven said, then, leaving the cloth on his forehead, covered his ears with his hands. "Need some help in here!" he called, his raised voice thankfully muffled.

So too was the voice of someone else who entered the room, the two of them conversing in what to Paris were nothing more than murmurs. But at least they were the only voices, the ones in his head from before blissfully quiet. Gone for good, he hoped. Now if the raven could just get rid of his pain too. More hands were laid on him, more voices in the room, then a chant began and memories of the monster returned.

He struggled where he lay, and the hands on him pressed harder, hotter, a wave of heat rolling from the tips of his toes up his body. Higher and hotter. "Help me," he pleaded with the raven.

The hand over his right ear shifted. "That's what they're trying to do. They're burning out the poison. Just hold on a little longer."

He stared up at the shifter asking for his trust. "Who are you?"

"Icarus sent us."

Guilt tore at his insides, sharper than any pain that tore at the rest of his body. "Is he—"

"Safe," the raven said with a wry grin. "You are too."

"My father?"

"Doesn't know where you are."

He'd look around if he could, but the raven's hands held his head steady, held him just out of the lake of fire that threatened, that inched higher with each chanted syllable. "Where am I?"

"With the Redwood Coven."

"Where? How far—"

"You're in Encinal. Near the shellmound."

Clear across Yerba Buena from the family compound of condos. Clear across the Bay too. On consecrated ground that surely his father was smart enough to avoid. He let out a relieved breath, and the ironic twist of the raven's lips smoothed into a soft curve Paris ached to paint.

Soft like the fingers that took up stroking his temples again. "Now, let the witches do their work."

"Don't leave me."

"I've got you."

As the heat rose, Paris closed his eyes and focused on the soft sheets beneath him, on the cool rag across his forehead, on the gentle fingers caressing his temples. Let the sensory anthesis carry his mind away while his body fought what he didn't fully understand yet.

The raven said he was safe.

He believed him. For now.

TWO

PARIS WAS LOST.

Wherever he was, it didn't look like any part of Yerba Buena he knew. Not Sunset Hill where he lived, not the Lakeside apartments where his best friends, Kai and Jason, stayed. Not Sutro Hill, the Lost Valley, the Manor, the Canyon Lands or anywhere in between. He'd been raised in YB, was familiar with every nook and cranny of his hometown. He was as much a child of YB's mist and hills as he was the only son of Vincent Cirillo.

This tree-lined street of single-family cottages did not exist in YB. And nowhere in his world was the sky above, the buildings around him, and the ground beneath his feet varying shades of violet.

Violet.

Something clicked. Like that instant in his favorite jazz tune when the first instrument on stage made itself known. A single spotlight on the piano, its notes high and lilting, calling to him.

For what, he wasn't sure yet.

He followed the street to the next intersection and glanced right—more houses—then left, spying what looked like a strip mall just up the street. They had those—and houses like those around him—in the suburban areas outside of YB, especially south in Portola.

Was that where he was?

He picked up the pace as he approached the shopping center. It was brighter than on the tree-lined street, but the violet hues persisted. They gave the pale bearded man in the grocery store apron a pale eerie glow as he shagged carts in the parking lot.

A shiver raced up Paris's spine. Another instrument joined the piano, a bass guitar with its deep, dark rhythm— a counterpoint.

A warning.

Paris hung back at the corner of the building, watching as the bearded man initiated a conversation with one man, then another who passed him in the parking lot. When a young woman approached the car he was closest to, he didn't speak. He just glared at her, his blue eyes burning with thinly veiled malice.

Worried for the woman's safety, Paris moved to step forward.

She whipped her gaze in his direction, and the boom of drums on Paris's mental stage drowned out his gasp.

Blond hair fell around the woman's bruised and battered face—her nose broken, her lip split, one eye bloody around a brown iris.

Human, then.

Her lips moved, but no sound came out.

That didn't matter; Paris could hear her in his head. Her

two words like the final instrument joining a quartet—the trumpet wailing.

Help me.

———

Paris woke with a start, in full-on panic mode, choking for breath, ears ringing, scrambling to push himself upright. His hand landed on something wet. Slipped. Then he slipped too, his limbs failing to hold him, the pain that shot through them too much to fight the tangled sheets and the gravity dragging him off the side of a padded table to the floor.

His elbow hit something metal on the way—a bucket that went skidding across the wooden floor—and Paris howled. Clutching his elbow, he flopped onto his back, unable to do anything else, and stared up through tears at a ceiling that wasn't his, the plain white drop tiles a far cry from the dark and starry night he'd painted above his own bed.

Footsteps rushed toward him, their vibration and sound finally cutting through the ringing in his ears. He twisted his head, found the door, and scurried as fast as he could on his back the opposite direction, grabbing the metal bucket as he went. He rammed against the far wall and twisted onto his side, clutching the bucket in front of him, the only protection he had against the bearded monster coming for him.

Only it wasn't the monster of his nightmares that appeared in the doorway. "Oh, hey!" said a stranger with tan skin and black hair. His wide eyes were black too. "You're awake." Something about him seemed familiar, the sharp nose, the thin-lipped smile, the long lanky limbs. If not for his height and black eyes, Paris might have mistaken him for Kai, but that wasn't right either. He approached cautiously, hands up, palms out. "I'm a friendly," he said as he kneeled in front of him. "How'd you get all the way over there?"

"Where am I?" Paris gritted through clenched teeth as he tried to use the wall to lever his torso upright.

The other man clasped his shoulder, steadying him and helping him the rest of the way to sitting. "I've got you."

I've got you.

"The raven," Paris croaked, the similarity clicking into place, the words reminding him of his rescuer. "Where is he?"

"He had somewhere else he needed to be." The stranger eased the bucket from Paris's white-knuckled grip. "He asked me to stay with you."

Hands free, Paris crossed his arms over his chest and came into contact with the bandages covering his arms. He glanced down at his legs peeking out from the sheets still tangled around his waist. Bandaged too.

All of it rough.

Like the woman's face from his dream.

Like the past however many hours of his life.

He wished he had the bucket back, nausea threatening. He tugged at the bandages instead, a distraction and an end to the immediate violence against his skin.

Long-fingered hands covered his. "You need to leave those on," the stranger said. "Your wounds are still healing."

He shuddered at the reminder of the searing heat. A sharp contrast to the cold floor beneath him and the cool wall at his back. He gathered more of the sheet around him, the chilly shock working its way inside.

"You're cold?"

He nodded.

The man stood and crossed the room to the cabinet that was near the door. When he returned, he carried a stack of gray clothing. "Icarus said to bring you these." He handed the soft sweats to Paris. "He said they would make you feel better."

His eyes watered again, and he clutched the clothing to his chest. The courtesan was always so good to him. Despite being a vampire, Icarus had never scared him, had never committed a single violent act against him. Unlike Paris, who had given his father's warlock Icarus's contact info, knowing nothing good could come of it, knowing their promises to keep Icarus safe were probably a lie, but having no choice, his father's knee on his neck at the time. He should've let him end it then.

A mug appeared in his periphery. "How about some tea?"

Paris accepted the cup, sniffed the drink inside, and, relatively confident it was just an herbal blend, sipped it slowly. It coated his throat and made it easier to get the words out. "Who are you?"

"Liam Kelley." He shifted out of his crouch and onto his ass, sitting cross-legged across from him. "Mac's brother."

"Mac?"

"Cormac. The raven."

The raven. The witches. More of it was coming back to him. "We're in Encinal?"

Liam nodded. "With the coven."

Paris could hear muffled voices, other movement in

whatever building they were hiding in. "What are they doing?"

"Packing. They tend to stay on the move."

Paris had heard that about the witches. He recalled the map in his father's command center, little green pins identifying each coven's location. Had there been one in Encinal? He couldn't say. Everyone knew the nearby shellmound was haunted. That the area was consecrated. But did Vincent know the witches hid nearby too? Would he find him here? "Where will I go?" he asked Liam.

"With them, for now."

He held the sweats closer, his whole immediate world. But what of the rest? "Can I get a phone?"

"'Fraid not. Mac's orders."

"I need to check on my friends. If my father—"

"Your father has his hands full right now. He probably hasn't even realized you're missing."

"But I was supposed to meet them. They'll be worried."

"It's the week before the Rift anniversary. I doubt they'll blink."

Harsh. "I like your brother better."

Liam's laugh filled the room. "You might be the first person who's ever said that." He stood and offered Paris a hand. "Think you might be able to eat something? Mac said it's probably been a while. You're human; magic will only get you so far."

The thought of food didn't turn his stomach the way it had earlier. Maybe the tea was helping. "I can try." He held the sweats in one hand and took Liam's in the other. It was warmer than Paris expected. "You're a shifter too?"

"The whole family is." Liam helped him to his feet and, once Paris was relatively steady, left him leaning against the wall. "Get changed, then give me a shout. I'll be right outside. Is there anything else you need?"

He shook his head, but just before Liam reached the door, an idea occurred to him. A distraction—an outlet—he'd welcome. "Liam," he called, and when the raven's brother turned, he added, "Paintbrushes."

Liam paused over the threshold, dark brow furrowed. "What?"

"Can I get some paintbrushes? And some paints, please. Any colors will do."

"Yeah," he said, smiling. "We can do that."

He disappeared out the door, and Paris exhaled, eyes closed, until the bruised and battered face of the woman from his dream appeared behind his eyelids again. "Purple!" he shouted, hoping it wasn't too late to amend his request. "I need purple paints."

THREE

PARIS GLANCED at the phone in his hand and thought Jason would be proud. Maybe even Kai a little too. Kai had worked smuggling jobs with Jason before he'd gone straight and become the best bartender in town. Paris doubted Jason would ever give up the life. Despite the danger, and despite Kai's frequent objections, the thrill of the steal kept Jason going.

Paris understood that feeling, today especially. A bolt of excitement had raced up his spine as he'd successfully picked the pocket of the witch who'd been fussing over him. It was a smaller device, ultra lightweight, not the heavy sort you'd immediately notice missing. Nevertheless, Paris figured he didn't have long.

He slipped around the corner of the building they were hiding in and checked the location of the sun. Close to the western horizon; it would be sunset before long. Kai would already be at work. Good, he wouldn't be there to talk Jason out of the favor Paris hated to ask. He flipped open the phone and punched in his friend's number.

"Hello?" Jason answered, sounding half asleep. "Who is this?" he asked, no doubt confused by the unfamiliar number.

"Jason, it's Paris. I had to borrow a phone."

"Paris?" Bed springs squeaked, and Paris imagined his friend wiping the sleep from his big brown eyes. "Where are you? We were worried when you didn't show at the club last night."

"Dad tried to kill me again."

"He *what*?"

"Monster, snakes, altar, it was a whole thing." He'd spent the better part of the day painting out his trauma on the walls of the makeshift infirmary where he'd been treated, which was the only reason he could mention the ordeal now without throwing up. "I'm fine," he added before Jason could work himself into a fury on his behalf. He'd stepped into the fray between Paris and his father before; he didn't have to this time. "Some of Icarus's . . . friends . . . rescued me. Are you and Kai okay? Did Dad or anyone come after you?"

"We're fine too," Jason said. "And no, we haven't seen your dad or any of his crew. But Paris, should we be worried? Do I need to go get Kai from work? Do we need to come get you?" His voice escalated in volume with each sentence, uncharacteristic anxiety pushing his devil-may-care friend fully awake. "What's going on?"

Paris rested back against the wall. "Dad probably thinks I'm dead. You should be fine too. I just needed to be sure."

"Where are you?"

"Encinal, for now, but I think we're moving soon."

"Shit feels weird, Paris. Something's going down."

"It's just the Rift anniversary," he lied to himself and his friend.

If the whole sacrifice thing didn't give away the weirdness, the ramp up in his father's operations would have. He'd spent most of his days in the command center, barking orders Paris could hear through the walls, usually at his pet warlock, Atlas, who Paris was beginning to believe didn't sleep given all his comings and goings.

"When will you be back?" Jason asked.

"I don't know. Dad needs to keep thinking I'm dead. Which is why I need to ask for a favor."

"What do you need?" Jason replied without hesitation.

"You know Maxine Hill?"

"The vampire who works the door at Club Sutro?"

"That's her. Her dad's human. He's in hospice at YB Gen. He doesn't have long, and she needs Daylight to visit him."

After the Rift, that day thirty years ago before he, Jason, or Kai were born, that Paris had only read about in the books his tutors brought him, when Nature and Chaos had gone to war with YB as the epicenter, hospice had become the most locked-down ward at any hospital. Too many nearly dead bodies that could be used for evil. Vampires were at the top of the list of excluded visitors, which was why hospice visiting hours were only during the day when vampires couldn't be out. Unless they'd ingested Daylight, a magic-brewed potion that Vincent kept on hand for his own army of vamps. And that Paris had pilfered small amounts of whenever the opportunity presented itself. Never enough for Vincent to notice, but enough for those who needed it, like Icarus had in order to protect someone he loved and like Maxine did to visit her dying father.

"And you've been supplying her," Jason said.

"I was supposed to deliver her next batch last night."

"Where is it?"

"In my private wine locker at Benton's."

Jason laughed. "You think they're gonna let me into a place like that? Breaking into your condo would've been easier."

He maybe had a point. Paris couldn't recall a single pair of jeans Jason owned that weren't ripped, and ripped denim was not the recommended attire for one of the nicest restaurants in town. But he also couldn't recall Jason ever meeting a lock he couldn't pick. "Jason."

His friend's laughter subsided. "What?"

"You're the best smuggler in Yerba Buena."

"Charmer." Paris could hear the smile in his voice. "How much does she owe you?"

"Tell her it's on the house for being late."

"You're a damn softie, Cirillo."

You're too soft.

"So I've been told." More times than Paris could count.

"That wasn't meant as an insult," Jason said, his voice gentle and sincere. "It's what makes you one of the best people I know. You help others, you protect them in your own way. You do the thing your dad promises and never delivers."

His friend's words chased away some of the chill that had wound back into his soul. Made him believe what he'd been doing was right. That he was right. Maybe he was soft, but that softness, in himself and the things around him, was how he survived the violence. Violence he was asking his best friend to step into.

"Jason, if it's too risky—"

"Didn't you just say I was the best smuggler in YB?"

"Thank you," Paris said with a small, relieved smile. "Give my love to Kai."

"Will do," Jason said. "And in case it's not obvious, I'm glad your dad didn't succeed. Love you, buddy."

"Love you too."

He flipped shut the phone just as the door behind him swung open, the witch from earlier poking her head out. "Oh, there you are."

"Sorry, just needed some air," he lied. "Paint fumes and all," he said, flashing his stained fingers on one hand while he clutched the phone with the other behind his back.

She knitted her brow, no doubt wondering about those non-existent paint fumes, but a call from inside saved Paris from having to lie his way out of his lie. "It's safer inside," she said, holding the door open for him. "Our protections don't extend beyond the walls."

"What about the crows?" he asked as he stepped inside. "They're all over the roof."

"Well, not all the protections," she amended before shutting and locking the door behind him. "Have you seen my phone?"

He shook his head, playing the fool everyone thought he was. She scurried past him, muttering to herself about always leaving things behind, completely missing the moment he slipped it back in her pocket to find again soon.

FOUR

"YOU NEED TO MOVE. NOW."

Paris recognized that deep, serious voice, though it was more strained than the calmer, softer version of several days ago. Hurried footsteps punctuated each word, the raven charging down the hall toward the room at the end Paris had claimed. And painted one whole wall of, from floor-to-ceiling, even the jamb around the door.

But before Mac could reach him, he was waylaid by Liam outside the room. "Where's the fire, brother?"

"Vincent hired someone to hack the coven's location. We're trying to slow him down, but someone made a call out from here. The witch whose phone was used said it wasn't her."

"Shit," Paris cursed as his brush slipped, smearing his guilt across the chin of the young woman from the grocery store parking lot.

A blink later, Mac appeared in the doorway, and Paris stumbled back against the wall behind him.

Eyes glowing violet, color high on his cheeks,

wrapped in nothing but a clearly borrowed trench that barely reached his knees, the raven was even more stunning than in Paris's hazy memories. He was tall and rangy like his brother, but bigger somehow. From the added definition of his lean muscles to the authority he carried himself with to the blue, black, and violet aura that pulsed around him—duty, loyalty, and regret, a terrible tangle, inside a barely there ring of red, pushed to the very edge.

Wait . . . He could sense auras? Since when? He hadn't noticed Liam's or any of the witches' before now.

"It was you?" Mac's bark snapped him out of his thoughts. "You risked all these people." He threw an arm out the direction he'd come. "Witches who brought you back to life. My brother who watched over you. I saved your s—"

"Thank you," Paris said, finding his voice and legs as he pushed off the wall.

Mac jerked upright and blinked, the violet of his eyes fading to black. "What?"

"Thank you for saving my life. I don't think I said that before."

Mac just stared, his mouth opening and closing several times before he pressed his lips together, seemingly stymied.

Chuckling, Liam stepped to his side and clapped his shoulder. "The appropriate response is *you're welcome.*"

"Get packed up" was no less appropriate, given the circumstances he'd described. Paris didn't hold it against him, especially as he'd hastened things along. Mac rotated back to the door, then wobbled to a stop, inhaling sharply. "What is this?"

Paris flashed his stained hands, the brush woven through his fingers. "It's how I deal."

Mac moved closer to the wall, his gaze roving over the violet-tinged murals. The small, bearded man in the apron to the left of the doorway. The monster with snakes dripping from his chin to the right. "This was the giant?" Mac said. "Before and after?"

"That's right," Paris said, fighting and failing to keep the shiver out of his voice.

Another step right, and Mac stood before the mural of the altar where Paris had almost died. His fingers hovered in the air, just above the wall, tracing the knives that jutted up from the altar into the painted Paris's back, then the wispy swirls around his head. "What are these?"

"The voices," Paris said, whisper-quiet, afraid that if he spoke of them any louder they might come back. "It felt like they were carving into me, then screaming in my head."

He paused only briefly in front of the raven with its wings spread and talons extended before stopping in front of the last figure. "Who's this?"

"After the witches did their thing," Paris said, then to Liam, "Right before I woke up yesterday and you found me on the floor"—he waited for Liam's nod—"I had a dream about her. But I think it was just me projecting so my brain could work it all out."

Mac jutted his chin at the painting of the clerk, then the one of the woman. "Take pictures," he said to Liam.

"Why?" Paris asked.

"Something about her is familiar," Mac answered, his gaze still fixed on her. "Why is it all in purple?"

"That's how I saw it in my dream."

Mac's head whirled around so fast, so like a bird's, that

Paris almost laughed. The shock—and alarm—in the raven's once again violet eyes stopped him. Made him gulp instead. He was thankful a witch leaned her head in the door and released him from Mac's assessing stare.

"We'll be ready to go in ten," she said.

"Where are we going?" Paris asked.

"You'll find out when we get there."

He shifted his grip on the paint brush, holding it in his fist like a weapon. Nothing the ravens or witches had done so far indicated they meant to harm him—quite the opposite—but still . . . "No offense, but unknown destinations have not worked out so well for me this week."

"He has a point," Liam said.

"You'll go with the witches to Calera," Mac conceded.

"And what about you?"

His face fell—that terrible tangled aura from earlier knocking Paris back a step. And if his aura hadn't, the wretched pain in Mac's voice would have. "I have to do something I've put off for too long."

Liam stepped in front of him, expression sympathetic. "Is there any way around it?"

"We're about to find out."

Liam drew his brother into a tight embrace and mumbled words Paris couldn't understand. "Ní hiasc é go dtí go bhfuil sé ar an mbanc."

Mac's gaze flicked over his brother's shoulder, catching on Paris's, and when he said, "I hope you're right," Paris didn't think it was only about whatever miserable duty was directly in front of him.

FIVE

TWINKLING ORBS of light led their caravan down a winding limestone road and through a dense grove of towering trees. The last car in front of Liam's turned off at another cabin, this one the same as the handful of others they'd passed—four green walls, a stone chimney, a shingled roof covered in moss.

"Is there another one back there?" Paris asked, peering into the darkness.

"One more," Liam said. "If memory serves . . ."

He drove them under a stand of trees whose branches had woven together over the road, and darkness swallowed them whole for an endless few seconds. And then they were out the other side, moonlight filtering through the branches to reveal a single cabin at the end of the road, barely visible among the tangle of green that stretched as far as Paris's human eyes could see.

Liam pulled the car into the gravel drive, and Paris stared out the windshield. "What is this place?"

He'd been born in the city, had rarely traveled outside it,

and never to any place like this. His world consisted of concrete, fog, and waves that crashed against sheer cliffs. The only thing remotely similar about this place were the breakers he could hear in the distance, from the direction they'd come along the ocean road. He'd thought they were going to the roadside motel by the coast, but they'd driven right past it and down the road that led to this forest. Or was it a jungle? Paris couldn't say, all of it new to him.

"Well," Liam said as he shoved his car door open, "when I was a kid, it was a campground." He waited for Paris to exit the car before continuing. "Then it was a resort property. Little cabins in the woods that the rich folk in YB and Portola could run away to."

"And then what?" Paris said as he grabbed his bag of borrowed clothes, bandages, and paint supplies from the trunk. "The moss won?"

Liam chuckled as he shouldered his duffel. "More like the Rift won, but yes, when people stopped coming out this way, Nature took over. Call it her anti–Canyon Lands."

Paris couldn't think of a better description. He rotated where he stood, inhaling deep and taking it all in. "It's beautiful."

"It's so dark out here you can hardly see."

"But it smells like life and the ocean, all rolled into one."

"Don't forget the rotting wood."

Paris glared in his direction, certain the shifter could see his rueful expression, even in the dark. "I'll amend. It smells like life and death, the *natural* kind. Nothing smells like this in YB."

"Fair enough." He fished a key out of his pocket and opened the door, holding it for Paris to enter first.

Into total darkness.

Paris extended an arm, searching cautiously for the nearest wall and, once found, backed himself against it, staying out of Liam's way. He moved around in the dark, seemingly undeterred, removing what sounded like sheets on furniture and stacking logs in a fireplace.

"You've never been to Talahalusi?" he asked from Paris's left.

"Dad forbade it." Shot him down every time he'd mentioned visiting the vineyards and farmlands north of Yerba Buena. But others had told him about the region. About the more temperate climate, the changes the governing Indigenous tribes had made to preserve their lands, the wash of colors so absent from YB, from the vegetation to the wine to the artwork. Jason had brought him sunflowers from there once, and Paris had spent months painting them in secret.

"It's like this," Liam said, drawing Paris out of his thoughts, with his words and the strike of a match. "But without the mustiness." Fire flickered to life in a corner fireplace, the flames casting enough light to make Liam visible again.

"That's where you and Mac are from?" Paris asked him as he continued to survey their surroundings. A stone hearth, a table, a rustic kitchen, and a couch and oversize chair. And if Paris squinted hard enough, a bed on the far wall and an enclosure in the far dim corner that he guessed was the bathroom. "Talahalusi?"

"Our family owns a vineyard up there. Monte Corvo."

"Mac works a vineyard?" Even if Liam weren't able see his face, Paris's voice—and the bag he dropped—would have given away his wide-eyed surprise. In no universe could he imagine the intense raven tending vines. "What's he do? Stomp the grapes?"

Liam laughed out loud, that same carefree guffaw from earlier that couldn't be more different than his brother's small, soft smiles. By the time his hilarity subsided, the flames had grown healthy, casting a warm glow about the cabin. But before Paris could get a better look, Liam's answer to his joking question stopped him cold. "No, Mac's a cop." Then sent him scrambling for the door. Liam beat him to it, blocking his path. "We know who you are, Paris. We know what you do."

"And what's that?" He hated the wobble in his voice, but there was no help for it. He was at a disadvantage—trapped in a strange place with a shifter, at the mercy of others who would use him against his father. Sure, they might have rescued him, but now that they had him, how far would they go to get information about his father's operations? His dad was right; he was a fool. He'd spent the past few days painting pictures when he should have been learning everything he could about his captors and plotting his escape.

"You're a dealer," Liam said. "You work small jobs for Vincent."

Paris whipped his gaze back to him. "I don't work for my father."

Liam stepped back, hands raised, palms out. "I believe you. Icarus vouched for you. And your dad tried to kill you. Evidence is in your favor."

"You talk like a cop too."

"I would be, if Mac let me." There was a resigned tilt to his smile, a wistfulness in his voice that Paris recognized. Dreams that someone else had quashed, though he suspected Mac's motives were more altruistic than his father's. Before Paris could question him further, Liam opened the door and left it that way while he gathered a stack of clothes from his duffel.

He was giving Paris an out. To who the hell knew where, but the gesture, the intention was loud and clear. Paris was free to go.

He stayed instead, sensing his chances were better with his rescuers than the man who'd repeatedly tried to kill him. "For what it's worth, I've never been on my father's side."

Nodding, Liam passed him on the way out the door. He didn't go far, just over the threshold to the outside bin on the tiny porch, stashing the stack of clothes inside it.

"Who are those for?" Paris asked.

"Me, after a shift." He glanced over his shoulder, a devilish smirk turning up one corner of his mouth. "Unless you want to see me naked."

"I'd rather see your brother naked—" Paris slapped a hand over his mouth, as if he could somehow hold in the words that had already escaped.

Liam rolled his eyes as he stood, but his smile gave away his amusement. "Is it the dark and broody of it all?"

"You've got dark hair and dark eyes too."

"But not the broody."

Paris shrugged as he followed Liam back inside. He hadn't known Liam long, but he didn't think the good-natured man had a broody bone in his body. And broody, for better or worse, was Paris's type, hence why he'd never fallen for Jason, whose ease and carefree attitude reminded him of Liam. And he'd never made a move on Kai because anyone with half a brain could see Jason and Kai were destined for each other.

"Tell me about him," Paris said as he sank onto the couch in the middle of the cottage. "Why is he all dark and broody?"

Liam claimed the oversize chair to Paris's left and propped his socked feet on the coffee table. "He's the oldest."

"That can't be all of it."

His gaze drifted past Paris to the fire and in the serious expression that crossed his face, Paris saw the resemblance to his brother beyond just their similar features. "He's the reaper for our clan."

"What does that mean?"

His dark gaze swung back to him, and in it was a hint of the violet Paris had seen in Mac's. "He carries souls to their ends."

Paris had read about ravens and other psychopomps who ferried souls. Had heard his father talk and brag about manipulating them to do his bidding. But Mac seemed to be heaping the torture on himself. "And he's a cop? That's misery on top of misery."

"You're not wrong, especially when it's the lost ones that keep him up at night."

Paris quirked his head, not quite following. "Lost ones?"

"Cold cases, that's his specialty. Souls he can't find. Icarus was one."

"Well, he found him now."

"And he may have to deliver him soon." Unmistakable sadness streaked through Liam's eyes before he averted his gaze again. "And a family friend too. It's almost as bad—"

He cut himself off and swallowed hard. "Mac's not in a good place right now."

And yet he'd rescued him and seen him to safety. Had made sure his brother looked after him, even after Paris had compromised their safety. "Is there anything we can do? To help?"

"What he asks." Liam pushed to his feet, then around the coffee table, headed toward the kitchen. "We stay here, safe and sound, until the coast is clear."

Paris twisted on the sofa. "What's happening to Icarus . . . to Mac's friend . . . it's because of my father, isn't it?"

"In part, but there's a lot more going on than just one evil man."

One evil man who was his father. Who Paris had unwittingly helped by giving him Icarus's contact info. Under duress, granted, but part of this was his fault. He'd find a way to do more; he had his own wrongs to rectify.

SIX

HUSHED, clipped voices teased the edge of Paris's consciousness.

He didn't try too hard to listen, didn't let them pull him out from under the flannel sheets and heavy quilt that chased away the forest's nighttime chill. Besides, convos he couldn't hear had become the norm. The witches had frequently visited the cabin, regularly checking in with Liam. They were always careful to talk in low, whispered tones, too quiet for Paris's human ears to discern.

He didn't take it personally. He was Vincent Cirillo's son. Why would anyone trust him? Liam had agreed to tell him if anything happened to Icarus or Mac, and in return, Paris had agreed to do what Liam asked, what Mac needed. Stay safe and out of whatever mess was going on in YB.

He thought maybe something major had gone down last night. He'd been outside behind the cabin, picking wildflowers for the vases he'd found under the kitchen sink, when the waves in the distance thundered so loudly it was like being back home, in his condo right on top of the cliffs.

And there'd been a weird energy to the forest around him, almost like it was vibrating.

He'd returned to the cabin and found Liam pacing from one end to the other, his typically relaxed manner vanished. But Liam had had no answers, just nervous energy, so Paris had put him to work kneading dough for the bread he'd wanted to make, the fireplace hearth too tempting to pass up. Then, after the dough had set the requisite time, he'd tasked Liam with babysitting it in the Dutch oven while he slept.

Which couldn't have been long, judging by the dim light behind his eyelids. Early morning, he guessed; definitely not time to get up yet. He yanked the quilt higher, aiming to pull it over his head, but then Liam's hand landed on his ankle, shaking it lightly.

"More sleep," Paris mumbled into his pillow. "Icarus and Mac okay?"

"It's me, Paris."

Sleep fled in an instant, Paris rolling onto his back and looking up into dark, haunted eyes. Mac's face was drawn, his shoulders slumped, the tan of his skin pale and his dark hair unruly. And his aura was an absolute train wreck. A speck of lighter relief, the red edge a tiny measure brighter, but darkness clawed at it—exhaustion, regret, sadness dominating.

Untangling an arm from the sheets, Paris reached up and palmed his cheek. It was so much colder than Liam's. "Are you okay?"

"I'm fine." Mac covered his hand but not to pull it away, as Paris expected. He nuzzled into it instead, as if he were searching for warmth, and Paris barely managed to swallow his surprise.

"What about Icarus and your friend?" Paris asked once he could make words again. "Liam said—"

A small smile teased the corners of his lips. "Also fine." He lowered Paris's hand, squeezed it, then stood. Paris recognized his clothes—dark jeans and a black sweater—from the stack Liam had put in the bin outside. "I have some news for you," Mac said. "Get dressed, and I'll meet you on the couch."

Paris wrestled free of the sheets and quilt and pulled on the sweats and hoodie he'd left by the bed. As he straightened, he noticed Liam was no longer in the cabin. He made a quick pit stop in the bathroom—no Liam there either—then ventured past the table to lay a hand on the loaf of bread wrapped in a towel, exactly the way he'd shown Liam to do it. The loaf was cool, taken out of the fire hours ago, the Dutch oven washed and drying upside down by the sink. "Was that you and Liam talking before? Did he leave?"

"He was needed at home."

"At Monte Corvo?" Paris said, and Mac cocked a dark, questioning brow. "He told me that's the name of the vineyard your family owns." Paris circled the chair and lowered himself onto the opposite end of the couch. "In Talahalusi."

"What other secrets did my brother spill?"

"He told me you were a reaper. Is that why you look so wrung out? Why you're cold? What happened last night? It felt . . . weird," he said, recalling his friend's too-accurate description.

Mac made a harsh sound, somewhere between a laugh and a groan, and drove a hand through his hair, disheveling it further. His gaze lighted on the waning fire and stayed there. "There was a battle," he said, tone as haunted as his eyes. "The first of many, likely."

"Right," Paris said. "As we get closer to the date of the Rift." It had happened that way every year for as long as Paris could remember. As mid-October approached, skirmishes between magical forces would escalate and most humans would plan their vacations out of YB accordingly. Well, most humans, except those like his father trying to profiteer from the madness. Sometimes the increased activity subsided after the Rift anniversary, sometimes it carried through to Samhain, and on several occasions, it had lasted all the way to winter solstice.

"It's different this time," Mac said. "Nature is back in the war."

Paris gasped aloud, no help for it. In all his tutors' lessons about the Rift, and in all the other books he'd read about it and the decades that followed, Nature hadn't been directly active in YB since that fateful October seventeenth thirty years ago. Her cause was still championed, otherwise places like this forest, like Talahalusi, like certain other parts of YB wouldn't exist. All of it would be like the Canyon Lands, which she'd ceded in the Rift, but in the battles and years since, she hadn't directly played a role. Until now. The weirdness both he and Jason had sensed.

"Last night," Paris started, "I was outside picking flowers, and there was this *energy* in the forest." He splayed his hands and wriggled his fingers, hoping Mac understood what he was trying to convey. "And the waves were so loud, even through the woods. It was like being back on Sunset Hill."

"She needed to pull the energy for what we had to do."

He shifted on the couch, angling toward Mac and

pulling up a knee, intrigued to the edge of his seat. "Which was what?"

"Save a phoenix from your father."

Paris jolted. "They exist? For real?" Phoenixes were mentioned in some texts, but they were so rare, so few and far between, their identities closely guarded secrets, that the stories and reports about them were a patchwork of myth and magic. No one was quite sure how they began or even how many remained alive.

"They do, and they belong to Nature, but your father and Chaos were hunting them."

Paris's wonder crashed in despair, his father ruining another joyful moment in his life. Not to mention all the lives he must have ruined in his quest for power. Paris gathered the nearest blanket around him, needing the softness to counter such violence. "You may not believe me," he said, "but I don't work for my father. I don't support his cause or Chaos. I never have."

"But you are his heir. And you told him how to contact Icarus."

"I didn't know what for. Just something to do with someone called the Devil, and they promised to keep Icarus safe." Paris leaned his forehead against his knee, eyes slipping shut as defeat and regret swirled in his gut. "And not that it matters, because I know I shouldn't have believed them and should have just kept my mouth shut, but they got that info with my father's knee on my neck. I didn't give it up voluntarily."

Mac's sharp inhale drew Paris's attention back to him, to the person who'd clearly been through hell the past few days but had still made sure he was safe and secreted away. Paris lowered his knee and inched out a hand, covering

Mac's where it rested on the cushion between them. "I'm sorry for what he's put you through. And I'm sorry he tried to hurt your friend and for whatever he did to Icarus. I don't want anything to do with him or his empire. He can keep it."

"You may not want it, but it's yours now."

Mac's gaze held his, the intensity of it momentarily distracting Paris from his words, but once they sank in, his breath caught. Made getting the most important question of his life out difficult. "Are you saying—"

Mac flipped his hand over under Paris's and gently held his. "Your father died in the battle last night."

Paris couldn't describe exactly what sound jumped out of his throat—a gulp, a shout, a gasp—it was the last news he expected. Tears welled in his eyes and raced down his cheeks, his chin wobbling so hard he had to wedge it against his chest.

Mac squeezed his hand. "I'm sorry."

"No!" Paris said, jerking his face back up. More than anything, he wanted this man, his rescuer, to know what he truly felt. "This isn't grief. It's joy, it's fucking relief I feel in my soul." The same sense of freedom he'd felt when Mac in raven form had landed on his chest on the altar. "For the first time in my entire life, I don't have to be afraid anymore."

He barely got the last word out when his sobs broke loose, twenty-plus years of pain and terror working their way up and out. Mac used the hand still in his to draw him into his arms, gathering the blanket around them both. Paris leaned against him, grateful for the steadiness, for the comfort while the awful world he knew fell away.

For his second chance at life to become a reality. Vincent would never hold him under the water again.

He could breathe, free and easy, and with that hopeful thought, the sobs began to subside until there were only sniffles and sizzling embers left. "He's really gone?"

Mac held him tighter, chin resting on the crown of his head. "I delivered his soul myself. Watched it get extinguished. I had to be sure. He won't hurt you or anyone else ever again."

"Thank you," Paris said, and yet the words didn't seem nearly enough. As he snuggled deeper into the raven's embrace, he silently vowed to spend the rest of his life earning his second chance. And to bring warmth and color into the life of the man who had given it to him.

SEVEN

PARIS WASN'T LOST this time.

He'd been here before. Would never forget sitting in the back seat of his father's SUV and crying over a future he'd never have. In retrospect, he'd probably been brought as a sacrifice that day, but it didn't make the day any less of a milestone in his past of painful losses.

Today looked much the same. The giant oval lawn full of people—a couple sharing a picnic, a group of friends tossing a frisbee, classmates chatting over books. The plaster and glass buildings with their echoes of mission-style architecture, the farthest north the trend had reached before magic and greed had chased the religious fanatics back south. Bright sun overhead, making the veneer of normalcy shimmer bright.

Portola University.

Paris would've liked to attend college, but erased persons, like Vincent had paid for him to be, couldn't enroll in school. Granted, he probably wouldn't have survived four years here. He would've been killed by a rival dealer or kidnapped by a tech oligarch to leverage against his father, but at least he would have been out from under Vincent's fist. Instead, Atlas had arranged for private tutors, all of them excellent and paid enough to get over their fear of working for the Cirillos. But that was as far as their connection had gone, none of them becoming friends. Paris only had Kai and Jason for that, and Icarus, whose company he'd paid for.

As a young man crossed in front of him on the oval, the glide of his steps too measured, the shift of his blue eyes too fast, the rise and fall of his chest nonexistent, Paris thought he must be a vampire like Icarus.

One with access to Daylight. Out here in the violet midday.

Violet.

Paris looked the direction the vampire had come just as the vamp glanced over his shoulder, both of them spying the small, bearded man on the oval's stone wall. Dressed in overalls, he sat munching on an apple, taking a break outside in the sun like everyone else.

But as the vampire moved to take another step and couldn't, Paris knew that wasn't what the man was doing at all. The vampire's claws extended, and he slashed at the monster's invisible hold. No one noticed his struggle except Paris. No one noticed the small man's red eyes or the snakes that slithered out from under his pant legs and sped through the grass in the vampire's direction.

No one noticed the world turn a deep, dark violet, or the oval lawn narrow into a deserted alley, or the vampire lying on the wet, grimy pavers with deep cuts in his arms and legs. No one heard him scream "Help me!" into the night.

No one except Paris.

———

"How, Paris? Tell me how to help you!"

Paris jolted awake, the dark, violet night resolving into a pair of dark, violet eyes. "Mac?" The raven's strained voice had echoed around the alley walls, pulling Paris out of Portola and back to . . . ?

A place that smelled of wildflowers, wood, and fresh-baked bread—as far away from home as Portola had been.

Tearing his gaze from Mac's, he planted a hand in the cushions and levered up to look around. A quilt-covered bed on the far wall, a half-eaten loaf on the kitchen table, a corner hearth blazing bright, a dusky green hue outside the windows. "We're still in Calera?" he asked, swinging his gaze back to Mac. "At the cabin?"

Mac nodded. "About ten hours later, but yeah, still here." He rocked onto his haunches beside the couch. "Where were you?"

"Portola." Paris hauled himself the rest of the way up and raked a hand through his hair, pushing it back off his forehead. "I can't believe I passed out like that. I'm sorry."

He gently patted his biceps, bandaged beneath the hoodie's sleeves. "You're still recovering."

Paris had removed the bandages on his forearms last night. Those wounds had mostly healed, but the deeper cuts in his biceps and thighs, the witches had warned, would take longer.

"And you got some big news this morning," Mac added.

"That you delivered, after I don't even want to know how long a night."

"It's not a competition, Paris." He stood and made his way to the kitchen. Out of the jeans and sweater and dressed in slacks and a dress shirt, barefoot and with his sleeves rolled up, he looked a hundred times more comfortable than he had in more casual clothes. "Coffee or tea?"

"Tea," Paris answered. "The olallieberry one, please." Mac threw a dark-eyed glare over his shoulder, and it took everything in Paris not to flip him the bird. Bird, heh. He settled for sass instead. "Don't judge. And *you* offered it."

"Only to be polite." One corner of his mouth twitched, fighting a smile, before he turned back to the kettle. "I'll let it slide since you make good bread."

Paris's insides warmed at the compliment, at the idea he'd been able to give Mac some comfort too. But it wasn't all his doing. "The starter for it was the witches', and your brother kneaded it, then babysat it while I slept," Paris said, as he pushed off the couch and headed toward the bathroom. "They deserve some of the credit."

A quick leak and bandage check later, Paris reemerged to two steaming mugs, bread and butter, and Mac waiting for him at the table. Also on the table was a stack of file folders Paris didn't remember from that morning. And come to think of it, those slacks and shirt Mac was wearing had not been in the stack Liam had put in the bin outside. "Did you go out when I was asleep?"

"Briefly. I met an associate at the motel down by the coast. She had some wheels and other supplies for us and the coven."

Paris peeked out the front window, to check out said wheels—a nondescript sedan—and to hide his grin that threatened, more of that earlier warmth intensifying and spreading out to his limbs. Mac had trusted him not to run.

"Where were you in Portola, in your dream?"

His grin died as he turned back to the table and slid into

the other chair. "You don't need to worry about those." The last thing he wanted was to burden Mac with more concerns—he had enough on his plate already—and especially for what would amount to nothing. "Like I said before, it's just me processing."

"I'm not sure it is." Coffee in hand, Mac leaned back in his chair, legs crossed, and repeated his earlier question. "Where were you in Portola?"

"The university."

And straightened in his seat.

"That's relevant?" Paris asked.

"Maybe. The monster from last week was there?"

Paris fought off his shiver with another sip of hot tea. "He was after a vampire."

"Icarus?"

Paris shook his head. "It wasn't him or any of my other clients. I didn't recognize him."

"Can you describe him for me?"

Knowing Mac was a cop, Paris recognized the interrogation for what it was, but if he hadn't known, he might not have made the connection, Mac gently drawing the answers out of him. More like a conversation between friends, but the raven never let a question go, circling back for the answer he needed. Paris would bet he was good with suspects and also with families of missing victims.

"He'd been turned at about my age. Midtwenties. Average height, slimmer build, dark brown skin, short, clipped hair, blue eyes, freckles over the bridge of his nose." Paris's gaze drifted out the window, summoning up the dream for anything else he'd noticed. "He knew he was being watched. And he didn't care. He was more concerned with getting out of there."

"Why do you say that?"

"He wasn't hiding what he was as he crossed the oval. It was full of people, and he was gliding too smoothly and not breathing."

"This was in broad daylight?"

Paris nodded. "As if he'd taken Daylight. I can paint him for you." His fingers itched to get to work, the walls of the cabin a blank canvas calling to him.

"And if you were to paint the giant, what would he look like this time?"

"Giant," Paris said with a harsh chuckle. "He looks nothing like that in his human form." He held his mug in both hands, close to his chest, guarding against the threatening chill. "In my dreams, he looks like he did when Dad handed me over to him. Incredibly average. You wouldn't notice him on the street. Short, skinny, frail almost, like his arms would shatter in a strong enough wind. Brown hair and beard, blue eyes that turned red when he froze the vampire, like he did to me when I tried to run. He's so small, the opposite of the giant he becomes."

"He was wearing a grocery apron when you painted him before. Was he wearing the same apron when he took you?"

"Not the same one, and he wasn't wearing any apron in this dream. He had on generic overalls, like a janitor or professional painter would wear." He lowered his mug and cupped his warm hands over his nape, head bowed. "The exact opposite of my father's suits. It's my brain, swapping one monster for another, one victim for another, but they're all me." Abused, chased, denied the bright, promising future he wanted and damned to dark, hopeless alleyways instead. "The scene changed," he told Mac. "From the oval to a dark alley where the vamp was cut open." He pushed his sleeves up and turned over his arms, the scars on his forearms fading but still visible. "Exactly like I was. He asked me to help him. It was just—"

"He's still alive, Paris."

His gaze shot up, along with his heart rate. "What?"

"The giant. He disappeared in that ball of magic he conjured." Mac pulled the top file off the stack, opened it, and pushed it in front of Paris.

The blond-haired, brown-eyed woman from the Portola parking lot stared up at him from a graduation photo. "Who is she?"

"Lola Duvall. She graduated Portola University, then went to work there as a systems engineer. She's from my stack."

"Your stack?"

"Of cold cases. She's been missing for over three years."

Paris's pulse galloped as his mind likewise raced, tying the pieces of his dreams to the pieces of the new reality around him.

To the raven sitting across from him.

"She's one of the souls you still have to deliver."

"Among others." Mac's gaze cut to the remaining folders beside him; Paris didn't think that was even close to the entirety of his stack. "You mentioned hearing other voices when you were on the altar. You painted them carving into you and swirling around your head."

"They were souls," he said, recalling more from that awful night, realizing now that that was how he'd thought of the voices then too.

Mac nodded. "I don't think you were the first being that giant sacrificed on his altar to Chaos. I want to know who he is and how many more souls he's taken. How many more humans like you and Lola he used to channel those souls through. I want to stop him from taking more. There's not much I can control in this war, but this—*this*—I can do. I need to do it. Will you help me, Paris? Will you help them?"

Help me, the vampire had begged him in that alleyway. *Help me,* Lola had pleaded in the parking lot. *Help me,* all those voices—souls—had screamed with him on that altar.

And now he had an opportunity to do just that. To make some good out of what had been the worst night of his life. To help those lost souls and to save others from being taken.

To help ease the burden of the man who'd saved him.

"Yes," Paris answered.

EIGHT

PARIS STEPPED BACK from his latest mural of the monster and tapped his paint brush against his hip. "I'm missing something."

He'd been working on the painting for hours, after the hours he'd spent painting both scenes of the vampire victim, from the oval and the alley. By now, it had to be the wee hours of the morning, nothing but pitch-black darkness outside, made more so by the roaring fire inside. Mac had kept the flames going while they'd worked—Paris painting, Mac searching his case files for clues and identities. They'd taken a break hours ago to eat the lentil soup a witch had brought over and the cheese sandwiches they'd grilled on the hearth, but Paris hadn't lingered long. Every minute away from his dream was a minute he risked losing details. Like whatever detail it was now that he couldn't put his paint brush on.

"Trick I learned for investigating crime scenes," Mac said as he stood. "Close your eyes and put yourself there but in the victim's shoes. Look at it from their perspective."

Paris recoiled at the thought. He'd lived it once himself already, had been a bystander each of the other times. Watching it from the sidelines, there'd been a veil between his fear and the victims', between him and the giant. He didn't want to be in his path again, imaginary or otherwise.

"I'm right here," Mac said as he slid a hand into the groove at the small of his back, resting it lightly there. "I won't let him hurt you."

Inhaling a shaky breath, centering himself with Mac's hand and the paintbrush in his own, Paris closed his eyes and put himself back on the grassy oval, ten or so yards from where he'd first stood in his dream.

When he glanced over his shoulder, he was directly in the giant's line of sight, and as his gaze locked with the monster's blue one, he realized it lacked the malice it had in the parking lot dream. When the giant looked at the vampire, he was hungry—for power. Paris recognized the look: it was the same hunger that had been ever-present in his father's eyes.

Instinct drove Paris to move the opposite direction, away from the threat, but the now red-eyed giant stopped him in his tracks, invisible bindings digging into his thighs and arms, into his existing injuries. Pain and fear spiked, and Paris struggled to breathe.

Until Mac's hand pressing gently at his back reminded him this was just a memory, a mental scouting mission like the real ones he used to go on with Jason. Turning fully around, he studied the giant, looking for anything he hadn't already captured with his brush. Finding nothing at this scene, he took another deep breath and moved on to the next one, putting himself on the ground in the dark alley.

Only he arrived sooner than when he'd been there the last time, the vampire's soul dragging him a few terrifying moments earlier. To when the monster leaned over him, so close Paris could smell rosewater, elderflower, and quinine on his breath and could see the scar beneath his beard. He'd been so out of it with fear when he'd been on the altar himself, he'd missed those clues before. Like he'd also missed the gilded knife with its topaz stone that the giant used to slice into the vampire's barely healed scars, the nick on the blade's edge causing Paris to scream right along with him, remembering the way his own skin had torn and shredded, the awful, hopeless—

A sharp tug at the center of his chest, his name repeated in calm, soothing tones, warm hands cupping his cheeks and soft fingers against his temples, drew him out of the alley and back to violet eyes. "There you are," Mac said from right in front of him, continuing to gently stroke his temples. His breath smelled of earth and cheese and the wine they'd drunk with dinner; not the terrible cocktail of his nightmare. "Just breathe for me."

"He took me back further," Paris said between gulps, his eyes filling with tears, the unexpected terror overwhelming, the crash landing back to relief jarring. "How? What's happening to me?"

Mac drew him into his arms, chin on his crown, holding him like he had yesterday, loose enough Paris didn't feel trapped but solid enough to feel safe. "We need to talk to the witches," he said. "But those knives you painted carving into your back, the voices in your head, I think whatever happened to you on that altar opened you up. He was channeling souls through you; he made you a medium."

Forehead against Mac's shoulder, Paris gasped for breath and tried to wrap his head around the most sensible explanation for the nonsensical. And worried who would come knocking next.

Next.

Two souls had already knocked, and he had new clues that could help them. He just had to pull himself together and share those with the detective standing right in front of him. Another deep breath, then he straightened and wiped the wetness from under his eyes. "He's toying with them for the hunt," he told Mac. "He captures them, then lets them go to chase them again. Lola's face was bruised and beaten, and the vampire had barely healed scars the giant ripped open again. But they were different too. He hated Lola. I don't know if it was personal or because she was a woman or because she was human, but there was malice there. With the vamp, he was after his power, plain and simple. He was hungry."

"That's good, Paris." Mac kept a hand lightly cupped around the side of his neck. "Means we need to look for prior connections and earlier abductions. Was there anything else?"

"He had a knife, gilded with a topaz stone. I can paint it. And his breath smelled like an elderflower tonic. The kind with rosewater."

"Only a few places to get that still."

"And he had a scar." He moved back in front of the monster's picture, grabbed the straight razor from his palette, and dipped the tip of his brush into the paint. He carefully dabbed a little onto the side of the monster's chin, swirled some to match the texture of the beard hair in that area, then, with the razor, thinned out the rest of the dab into a raised line, keeping it perfectly straight like the scar he'd seen. "Right there."

Mac moved closer, snapping pictures with his phone. "Oral or jaw surgery wouldn't leave a scar like that. Those surgeries are done inside the mouth. That scar is from an external injury, and with it being that straight, it was professionally treated. This is good, Paris," he repeated. "Real good."

"Assuming he's not erased, like I am."

Mac patted his shoulder on his way back to the kitchen table, opening his laptop and connecting his phone to various cables. "That's why multiple leads are important. There may not be surgical records, but someone sold him that tonic. I'll get the searches running."

"How do you even get a signal out here?" Paris asked as he dabbed his brush into more paint to get started on the knife. A small generator behind the cabin provided enough electricity for hot water, plumbing, a fridge, and a few other appliances, but Paris found it hard to believe Mac's computer transmitted with any reliability from these woods.

"Boosters and other tech." He gestured at the various attachments connecting the devices. "Icarus's sister is a hacker."

Paris bobbled his brush, flinging paint farther afield than he intended. "Icarus has a sister?"

"Adopted. They were in the same foster home."

"Huh, I knew he needed the Daylight to protect someone, but I never knew who." He swept his paintbrush so as to hook the tip of the knife's blade, then used his razor to shadow its peaks and valleys and create a nick in the straight edge. He winced, but shook off the thought before the remembered pain drowned him again. "Did my list of Daylight clients turn up anything? I didn't know the vamp from my dream, but maybe someone else did. Sometimes who I sold to wasn't the end user."

"Nothing in the hard files, but I have searches running against the digital." After a final flurry of keystrokes, he slumped back in his chair. "Why did you deal?"

Do deal, Paris almost corrected, but bit his tongue instead. He lifted his brush long enough to shrug, then after another swipe through the paint, continued to work on the knife's handle. "Folks needed it. Folks like Icarus. They all had good reasons."

"They could've been lying."

"I'm sure some were. Everyone knows I'm gullible, but if I was able to help one person, then I did what I could."

"While stealing from your father."

He dipped his brush in the yellow paint, added the touch of purple that tinted all his dreams still, then filled the hole he'd left for the stone in the middle of the handle. He used his razor again to clean up and define the edges, depicting a slight filigree to the border around the stone. "He promised to protect them, and he didn't." Paranormals would hire his father for protection, and the next thing the shifter or vampire or warlock knew, they were doing Vincent's dirty work for him. He was human, yes, but a monster in his own terrifying way. It was a business model, a hoard of stolen power and riches that Paris wanted nothing to do with. "What does it mean to be his heir?"

"I don't know yet. That's what I sent Liam to find out.

He'll recon with Adam and Icarus and the rest of the team, then report back."

Paris turned to ask who exactly was the rest of the team, but Mac's mouth stretching wide in a silent yawn made him yawn too since he, unlike his father, wasn't a sociopath. "When's the last time you slept?" he asked the raven, who tipped back his head and laughed, a tired, resigned thing that Paris felt all the way to his bones. "Go to bed, Mac."

He righted his head, a challenging, devastating smirk turning up one corner of his mouth. "Only if you do."

"Deal." He tossed his razor on the palette, capped his paints, and rinsed his brush in another mug he'd claimed for paint water, before ducking into the bathroom to wash his hands and check his bandages. When he reemerged in his tee and boxers, Mac was spreading a blanket on the couch.

"I said *bed*. You're way too tall for that sofa, and this bed is big enough for you and me and two more people."

Mac eyed the couch, looking anywhere but at Paris. "I'll be fine here."

Paris pressed his lips together and waited, hands on his hips, for Mac to glance up and meet his no-you're-not glare. He caved almost immediately, chuckling as he snatched up the blanket and headed for the other side of the bed. "I see why you and Icarus are friends."

"We're nothing alike," Paris said as he crawled under the sheets and quilt. "He's all strong and bossy and sexy."

"There's more than one interpretation of those words." Mac stretched out on top of the quilt, fully dressed, the blanket tossed over his feet. Paris let him have that distance, counting it a win that he was beside him at all, that he would get the good night's sleep he deserved.

Counted it a bonus when Mac turned on his side to face him, his dark hair falling across his forehead and making him look years younger. Sweet, almost. His words were even sweeter. "You're both good people. I didn't believe it about either of you at first, but like him, you keep proving me wrong."

Paris would have liked to stay in that gooey good place, but the ache in his heart wouldn't allow it. "Is Icarus really okay? He was always good to me. I'll never forgive—"

Mac's hand covered his where it rested between them. "He's fine. So is Adam. For what it's worth, you helped bring them together."

"Adam's the Devil, right? He's a phoenix?"

"Was. Like Icarus was a vampire."

Shock sent Paris levering up on his elbow. "He's not anymore? How did that work?"

Chuckling, Mac tugged him back down. "They were counterbalances—walking rebirth and walking death—whose souls became entwined. Mated, for lack of a better word. Nature released them both, channeling the magic back to her, and giving them a second chance. Their souls chose to come back together."

That did not sound like an easy task for the reaper who had to guide them. "And how did that work for you?"

Mac closed his eyes, but not fast enough to hide the wretched melancholy that streaked through them. He rolled onto his back and folded his hands over his middle. "We do what the souls deserve. Adam and Icarus deserved that second chance."

Paris started to reach out, but stopped himself short. "Do you want to talk about it?"

"I told—"

"What *you* felt?"

His Adam's apple bobbed, a hard swallow, then a single tear escaped the corner of his eye and raced toward the dark hair at his temple.

Fuck it.

Paris was a tactile person, and it was killing him not to try to soothe the obviously upset man—friend—beside him. He scooted closer and laid a hand on his shoulder. No words, just contact, letting Mac know he wasn't alone.

He found his words again after another swallow. "When you know the person on your list, when you love them"— he tapped his chest with his fingers—"it's a special kind of hell. What I want to happen and what must happen aren't always the same."

"Your aura was a wreck that day in Encinal and when you first showed up here."

He whipped his face Paris's direction, glassy eyes wide. "You can see auras?"

He withdrew his hand, tucking it back with the other beneath his pillow. "I couldn't before. I don't know why I do now, and I don't know how I know what they mean, but I do. Assuming I'm doing it right."

"What did you read in mine?"

"Loyalty, duty, regret."

He returned his gaze to the ceiling. "You were reading it right."

"What do you regret, Mac?"

"So much."

The words were faint, barely audible, but no less a wrecking ball for their hushed volume. They might as well have been a shouted cry for help, and it was everything Paris could do not to close the scant distance between them and to wrap himself around Mac like he'd done for him twice now, but he sensed even this was more truth than Mac let most people see. Balling his fist under the pillow, he forced his instincts back and waited Mac out, doing what he could to comfort with his presence and breaths. Eventually, Mac's slowed to match his, and after another minute, he turned back onto his side, facing Paris, hands tucked under his own pillow.

"We'll ask the witches to help you with the auras."

"I don't want to get rid of them. I think I'm supposed to see them."

"To help you understand them. Read them." He smiled softly. "For when they're not as obvious as mine."

"Thank you."

His eyelids seemed to grow heavy, slipping closed as he muttered "Welcome," and a moment later a light snore slipped out from between his lips. He shifted onto his stomach, close enough Paris could feel the puffs of his snores across his own face, could watch as the tension flowed out of his muscles. Finally, at rest.

But Paris was more awake than ever. His gaze wandered past Mac to the murals on the wall. They came to life in the dancing firelight, as did all the questions Paris still had about the people in them. Who was the monster? Who was the vampire? Why were he and Lola targeted? How could he help Mac deliver them? And why did he always see them in purple?

"The auras?" Mac mumbled, eyelids fluttering, and Paris realized he must have asked that last question aloud. And that Mac wasn't completely asleep yet.

"No, the souls."

That sweet, soft smile flitted over the raven's lips again.

"Because I do." Then disappeared into the pillow as he nuzzled down, surrendering fully to sleep.

And if Paris hadn't already started surrendering some of himself to this man, the tug he felt between them told him it was only a matter of time before he was ready to surrender it all.

NINE

THE RISING sun had just begun to filter through the forest canopy when Liam's car pulled beside the sedan in the cabin's gravel drive.

"Didn't expect to see you up so early," Liam said as he shoved open the car door.

Paris stood from where he sat on the front stoop and zipped his hoodie against the morning chill. "Couldn't sleep." It had been a fitful few hours for him, his mind never fully slowing, his heart more tangled than it had any right to be, his body wising up to the fact there was an unfairly attractive one beside it. By contrast, Mac had slept like a rock. Paris would have worried him dead if not for the steady rumble of snores. "Your brother is still asleep."

"Thank fuck." Liam rested back against the hood, hands shoved into the pockets of his parka. "We were worried about him. No one could remember the last time he'd slept."

"Can you take me to the coast? I haven't seen the water in days."

Liam took his non sequitur in stride, waving a hand toward the sound of crashing waves in the distance. "You can hear it."

Not good enough for Paris, for multiple reasons. He gave Liam the simplest, most persuasive one. "I was born and raised in YB. I looked out my window and saw water every day. I don't know how to be away from it."

"Mac will freak if he wakes and you're gone."

"I left a note." Two of them, in fact. In case he missed the one on the pillow beside his, there was another one under the edge of the kettle, next to the leftover bread. "But I don't think he'll be waking anytime soon. We only went to bed a few hours ago."

Liam cocked a brow.

Paris rolled his eyes and hoped it distracted from the blush heating his cheeks. "I was up painting, and he was working. Once we started competition yawning, it was all downhill from there."

Laughing, Liam pushed off the car. "All right, but let's make it quick."

The cabin was a short ten-minute drive to the water, owing largely to the twists and turns of the forest road. Paris didn't mind; the forest was magical in the light of day. He counted five cabins in addition to his, and an endless variety of trees, though redwoods and cypresses dominated. He also spied a knee-high patch of wildflowers in a sunny gap between the trees that he made a mental note to revisit, the meadow so unlike anything back home.

Or what was left of it. "What's it like back there? In YB?" he asked once they turned onto the coast road.

"More unstable than I've seen it since the Rift."

"You were alive for that?" Liam didn't look much older

than thirty, Mac like he'd be in his early forties, but it was impossible to tell with shifters.

"I was in college," Liam said, proving Paris's point. "Mac was already a cop and the reaper for the clan."

So however old they'd been, plus thirty years, longer than Paris had been alive. He suddenly felt very, very young. And very, very in over his head.

"It's a good thing you're out. Any humans should be."

Like his best friends, who had also claimed a spot in his worried heart last night. They were the other reason he'd asked Liam to bring him out to the coast. As his unwitting accomplice found out as soon as they stepped onto the ocean cliffs, the waves pounding below. "I need to borrow your phone," Paris said, his hand out.

"You know the rules."

"Look, you and Mac have this whole network to keep us protected, to watch our backs. My friends only have me, and for years, they were the only ones who had mine. They don't have the means or money to just get out of YB. Not everyone has the privilege to flee a war zone." Paris intended to flex his privilege, to offer Jason and Kai a means out, assuming he could get his hands on his trust fund still. And assuming his friends would take the offered help, unlike every other time he'd offered in the past. But he still had to try, especially with the stakes so high now.

Liam looked back the direction of the cabin, up and down the deserted beach, at the crashing waves below, before finally turning his knowing gaze back to Paris. "That's why we came out here, isn't it? So Mac wouldn't hear you."

"In part, though I really did need to see the water."

"Fuck," Liam said as he slapped the phone into his hand. "He's got his hands full with you."

Paris didn't think too hard on what Liam meant, instead turning on his heel and punching in Kai's number.

"Hello?" his friend answered.

"Kai, it's me, Paris."

"Paris—fuck," he cursed, voice lowered. If Paris had to guess, his friends had fallen asleep cuddled together, as was their way. The snick of a closing door, Kai's voice back to normal volume when he spoke again, confirmed as much. "We've been worried."

"I'm fine. Are you and Jason—"

"We're good, but Paris, there's something I need to tell you."

By the appropriately somber tone of his words, Paris knew where this was going. He spared Kai the trouble. "My father's dead, I know."

"I'm sorry."

"It's weird." He spoke freely with his friend who knew as much about him and his circumstances, about the abuse his father had regularly doled out, as anyone. "I appreciate it, because I know you mean that condolence for me, not because he's actually gone, but . . . I'm not sorry, Kai. I don't know where I go from here, what it means to be the only one of my family left . . ." The heir, another thread that had kept him awake, a convo he needed to have with Mac and Liam. But it didn't change the basic premise, the underlying relief he felt, the same kind of calm he got from staring out at the wide expanse of the ocean. "I'm not sorry he's gone. I'm not sorry that we're all safer for it."

"Are you?" Kai asked. "Safe? Wherever you are . . ."

He glanced over his shoulder, catching sight of Liam

strategically positioned to watch his back. "I'm safe, and I want you and Jason to be too."

"We'll be fine. I'm keeping an ear out at the club, and I get paid middle of the month. Jason was talking about some job too. We'll get enough money to get out before the seventeenth if we need to."

"I can send you money now."

"Thank you, but we'll manage."

As he'd expected. And he apparently didn't have time to argue either, Liam making a wrap it up gesture. Another car was pulling into the lot where theirs was parked, and them being seen out here probably defeated the point of being in hiding. "Fuck, I need to go. Listen, if you or Jason need me, I'm in Calera. About a mile past the ocean road motel, there's a road that leads up the hill, away from the beach and into the forest. We're the last cabin on the road. If you need backup, if you need anything, you come to me."

"You do too much for us." Kai's voice was as gentle and earnest as he was. He really was the best of them.

"I wish you'd let me do more. Love you both."

"Love you too."

He hung up and returned the phone to Liam. "Thank you. That was important to me. They're important to me. I needed to make that call."

"You're welcome. Now let's go before my brother sends out a search party."

One last, longing stare at the water, one giant inhale of salty ocean air, then Paris turned on his heel and followed Liam back to the car so he could get back to the forest and the soul waiting for him there.

TEN

MAC WAS SITTING on the front stoop when Liam pulled the car into the driveway. Barefoot, in the same wrinkled slacks and shirt he'd fallen asleep in, Mac clearly hadn't changed, and judging by the wild state of his black hair, he'd spent every minute since waking plowing his hands through it.

"Good luck with that," Liam said, and no sooner had he turned off the car than did Mac vault off the step, charging their direction.

Paris barely got his car door shut before Mac was there in front of him, backing him up against it. "Where'd you go?"

For all the bluster and violet swirling in the raven's eyes, Paris didn't feel an ounce of fear, not like when his father used to loom over him. His dad's posturing had been about power, control, and cutting him down; Mac's was the polar opposite, his aura pulsing with genuine concern and palpable relief. He was overreacting because he cared—about Paris.

Who stood taller for it, squaring his shoulders and lifting his chin, no fear of a backhand greeting his response. "The coast, like my notes said. Did you find them?"

"Both of them." He erased the scant distance between them and cupped the side of his neck like he had last night, but this time, Paris sensed, for his own comfort, Mac's thumb pressed against his pulse point. "But I didn't have a sample of your handwriting. I couldn't be sure it was you. That you hadn't been taken."

"I texted you," Liam called from behind the open car trunk.

Mac whipped his head to the side, frustration bubbling over in a growl. "Which could have also been faked."

Paris covered Mac's hand with his, holding his palm against his throat, making sure he could feel his heat, his heartbeat. "I'm right here."

Mac's gaze shot back to his, and Paris startled at the naked emotion in his dark eyes. The earlier concern and relief were still there, duty like always, but there was also a depth of loss Paris recognized all too well, the same sort of gaping hole in his chest where his mother lived. His absence this morning had tiptoed too close to that hole for Mac, whomever it was who'd torn it open.

"I'm sorry," Paris said, squeezing his hand. "I won't scare you like that again."

"Could use some help back here with these paint cans?" Liam called, and Mac spun on his heel with another growl that sent heat spiraling down Paris's spine. The last thing Mac needed to deal with was his bubbling crush, but if the raven kept giving him such raw glimpses and sexy growls, there'd be no stopping it from going supernova.

Shoving that distinct possibility aside for now, Paris

followed his curiosity to the back of the car. "Why are there paint cans?"

"To paint over the murals when you're done," Mac said. "I assume you don't want to relive those nightmares any longer than you have to."

What was that about an impending supernova? At this rate, it would arrive by nightfall. Paris closed his eyes, took a deep breath, and willed his libido back under control. He waited until Mac's tread hit the front step, putting him far enough out of visual range, before opening his eyes again and grabbing the remaining bag of groceries out of the trunk.

Inside, Liam was already peppering Mac with updates. "She's got a line on two more phoenixes. One that's in hiding, another that Vincent was bleeding dry."

"Is she following the vamps' internet chatter?"

Liam nodded. "They think it's an out, after what happened with Adam and Icarus. Bite a phoenix, be reborn."

"They missed that whole soulmate thing."

"Not to mention a reaper willing to risk his life to pull them back."

Paris dropped the bag of foodstuffs on the kitchen counter, his head spinning like the acorn squash that went rolling. His many hours spent dribbling a soccer ball indoors saved it from splattering on the floor. "Rewind," Paris said as he flipped the squash up into his hands. "My father was bleeding phoenixes dry? That's why he was hunting them?"

"For their power," Liam said as he claimed one of the table chairs.

"We think that may have been who Atlas disappeared with," Mac said, adding more insensibility to the pile.

"Atlas is alive? And gone where? He didn't take over?"

"He vanished from the scene where your father was killed."

"And Adam said none of the captured are talking," Liam relayed. "About who he disappeared with or anything."

Paris continued to put away groceries as his mind raced. Atlas had been his father's number two and his lover, the blond-haired, green-eyed warlock rarely far from his father's side. His father even had a door that led from his bedroom into Atlas's. Most people, including Vincent, had assumed Atlas was in his thrall, but Paris had never believed that. Atlas hadn't struck him as inherently evil nor weak enough of mind or magic for any human to exert such power over. A climber, yes; a monster, no. He'd always made sure Paris was taken care of, from tutors to nurses, and Paris had worked with him on more than one occasion to do the same for those Vincent had manipulated into working for him, cleaning up broken morale and broken noses. Paris had always thought the warlock was just biding his time until Vincent fucked up and got killed, and then he would take over because no one expected Paris to.

Had he actually stayed at Vincent's side all those years because of the person he'd escaped with? They may never know, but Paris did know he wouldn't let all the groundwork, all the connections Atlas—and he—had made go to waste. He folded up the empty grocery bag and rested back against the kitchen counter. "What if I could turn some of them to our side?"

Liam's "Them?" collided with Mac's "Our side?"

"The captured," Paris clarified. "What if I could sway them to Nature's cause? Convince them to give you whatever info about my father's organization you need?"

"It's not safe for you out there," Liam said. "With your father and Atlas both gone, there's a power vacuum in YB. He left behind a lot of money and a lot of banked power and resources that a lot of nasty people are after, human and otherwise."

Paris pushed off the counter, arms spread wide. "But I'm the idiot son. Everyone knows I'm worthless. My own father tried to sacrifice me. Why don't they just take it? They can't seriously think I'm a threat."

"A second ago you implied you weren't worthless," Mac said as he peered at him with shrewd investigator's eyes. "That you have some sway over the people in your father's organization. Someone out there"—he pointed at the window, at the world outside their bubble—"will also want to play that angle. And not for Nature's cause."

"You are the heir," Liam said. "You are target number one for those people trying to climb to the top."

"I can give you a list," Paris said, approaching the table. "Set up a meet." Mac opened his mouth to no doubt object, and Paris held up a hand, pleading his case. "They're not all bad people. Vet them first if you need to. You'll find out my father had a knee to their necks too."

"I can take the idea back to her and Adam," Liam said. "See if it's something they'll entertain."

Paris didn't know who *her* was, but she wasn't the one he needed to convince right now. He circled the table and kneeled beside Mac. "Whatever we're in the middle of didn't end with my father's death. We've got the Rift anniversary, Samhain too, and possibly solstice." He laid a hand on Mac's knee and waited for him to lay his own over it. "You asked me to help you. Let me."

ELEVEN

"SHOULD YOU BE HERE?" Paris asked as he dotted sea foam onto the sandy shore he'd spent all morning painting. It had been two days since his outing to the coast, and as much as he loved the earthy forest and colorful wildflowers he'd plucked from the meadow, he missed the water more. He'd needed to see it today, even if only on the cabin walls.

Mac's furious pen strokes at the table behind him stopped. "What?"

"I get the sense you're kind of a big deal." He lowered his brush and glanced over his shoulder. "Should you be here babysitting me and working this case when there's clearly bigger things going on?"

"You're kind of a big deal too," Mac said with a wry grin.

Paris couldn't decide whether to paint him with that crooked smile, the one that reminded him of the raven, or with the soft smile that Paris had woken up to in Encinal, the same one that would flit across Mac's face in the split second before he fell asleep.

Paris turned back to his mural. "Yeah, for being a sitting duck." And because he felt on the edge of hilarity and insanity, restless to the point of ridiculous, he swiped his brush through the yellow paint and added a rubber ducky on top of the breakers. "I'm just out here in the woods, painting pretty pictures and making you listen to music you probably don't even like." The quiet had been a peaceful respite the first few days here, but he was used to constant comings and goings, the sounds of the city, and the crashing waves below his condo. He'd cracked yesterday and asked Mac if one of his devices had enough juice to stream his favorite jazz channel. It had also been the music playing right before he'd been taken by the giant. He thought maybe it would jog his subconscious. Would help him put some of the channeling techniques he'd been working on with the witches to good use. No such luck. "I haven't even had another dream."

"One, I like the music. Two, finding Icarus was a cold case you helped solve."

"Not on purpose," Paris said as he gave the ducky two beady, black eyes and an orange beak.

"You still did. Three, we're following up on your list of potential informants in your father's organization. And four, as to the case we've been working, we've identified ten missing persons who may be connected to the giant who took you."

He tossed aside his brush and wiped his hands on the sweats he'd sacrificed to the paint gods days ago. "But we still don't know who or where he is." He slid into the chair beside Mac and gestured at the spread folders. "Or where all these poor people are buried."

"If they're buried at all. The vampire in your dream was eviscerated. The altar you were on was incinerated. You would have been ash if we hadn't rescued you."

"So there was nothing else in the area? No clues, no souls, no other evidence of the mystic or mundane?"

"Nothing. Just you and your dreams."

Propping his elbows on the table, Paris scrubbed his hands over his face and groaned. "Make it make sense, Mac."

"Okay, let's start from the top," he said, and Paris was glad his hands were still over his face. They muffled his chuckle at the very detective-like opener. "He was a giant," Mac continued. "Going by your dreams and my case files, he hunted from Portola all the way up to Talahalusi. He and the three other giants we know of in that range are allied with Chaos, and history indicates they are most active in the run-up to Samhain, when they make a coordinated offering in an attempt to open the veil and bring Chaos all the way through."

Paris shivered. "It was there that night. The darkness had already started to push through over the altar."

"Meaning the veil is particularly weak there."

"In the Canyon Lands? No shit, Mac, I could've told you that, and I'm just a human."

Mac's answering laugh was cut short by some realization, his brows snapping together as he yanked the files closer. "We know he needs a human to channel the souls through for his offering." He tossed aside three folders, reducing the number to seven. "These are the missing humans." After a flurry of keystrokes on his laptop, a map appeared, seven dots stretching from Talahalusi to Yerba Buena to Portola. "And where each lived when they were taken."

"Can you add dates?" Paris asked. "Each time they were taken. And add mine." The earlier deduction about the giant hunting and toying with his victims had significantly narrowed their pool. "Color them by year. I need the painting to come together."

And it did, Paris recognizing the pattern. "He hunts a few years in one place, then moves," he said. He pointed at the cluster in the south. "Lola and two others in Portola three to five years ago." Then to the group up north. "Two potential victims in Talahalusi seven to ten years ago." Then to his home. "Three in YB the last two years."

"But we don't know for certain that's the only place he's hunting," Mac said. "We rarely have more than one per year in my files, and we know the giants make sacrifices all through the month."

"But if the pattern holds," Paris argued, "he's in YB this October. He took me from YB."

"But he didn't hunt you. What if . . ."

Paris gestured with a rolling hand for him to spit it out.

"What if you were a substitute? What if someone got away . . ."

"They're still out there, then. And he's still hunting them."

"In YB, if you're right." Mac's fingers flew across the keyboard. "We need to see who else has gone missing recently. Whoever it is, they haven't hit my pile or my list yet."

An arching flame in the hearth brought another question to mind. "If he catches them," Paris said, "where would he take them? You said the altar I was on is gone. Are there other ones?"

"Rumored," Mac said, as he opened another map on screen. "In other places where the veil is thin."

Paris pointed at the one closest to the coast, not far from where they were now. "That one's close by."

Mac nodded. "Along the fault ridge between Portola and the ocean."

"We need to go there. See if there's any activity."

Mac's "Paris" reminded him of Kai's reply to some of his and Jason's more adventurous schemes. But in those cases, he and his friend were two humans getting into trouble way above their heads. This time, Paris had a well-connected raven at his side.

"Would I be in danger down there?" he said, pointing at that spot along the ridge. "Like I would be in YB?"

The dark-eyed glare cast his way was epic. "You're asking to go to a giant's altar."

"Okay, dumb question," Paris conceded. "Better one, how fast can you get someone from the team down here to go with us?"

The wry grin reappeared, and Paris decided that was the one he wanted to paint. "Liam, of course, and there's a shifter on our team from around these parts. And if I know her girlfriend, she'll come too." He raised a hand, quelling Paris's rising hope. "*If* Adam can spare them."

Fair enough. Bigger things and all that. "Deal."

TWELVE

THE NEXT MORNING, Paris stood in the middle of a deserted parking lot, zero gravel left underfoot, just knotty roots and rambling weeds covering the small unmarked area at the edge of the woods. He strolled across the similarly deserted road to the vista overlook on the other side. He glanced right toward where the ocean should be in the distance, then left toward where Portola should be, and saw nothing in either direction but the soupy gray mist that had made their drive up this mountain a terror Paris had no desire to ever relive. "Is it always this foggy up here?" he asked Mac, who was unloading gear from the car. "This is as bad as the Canyon Lands."

"Along the ridge here, yes," Mac said, as he shut the trunk. "Especially this spot. When I was a kid, there were rumors these woods were haunted." He crossed the road to stand beside Paris and pointed down the mountain toward Portola. "There's a lake down there you can't see for the fog, but before it was a lake, it was a bustling village. It flooded in one of the wars long before the Rift, when Chaos sent fire over the mountains and Nature countered it with waves. No one survived."

"Is it actually haunted here?" Before Mac could answer, a *Kraa* sounded overhead, a raven soaring out of the fog and onto a nearby branch. "Liam?"

Mac nodded as more black-feathered birds filled the trees, their *Kraa*s and *Caw*s joining the chorus, until their song was drowned out by the roar of a motorcycle cresting the ridge, dislodging loose pavement from the edge of the road as it swung into the lot beside Mac's car. Paris was so distracted by the stunning vintage bike—gas-powered, a rarity—that he didn't think too hard about the familiar movements of the backseat rider as she dismounted. It wasn't until she pulled off her helmet, dark hair falling around her tan face and delicate features, that Paris recognized her.

"Shit!" He turned to run and cursed again at the cliff blocking his escape. Which one was more likely to kill him —the fall or the mountain lion shifter?

Mac grabbed him by the back of the jacket, yanking him away from the edge. "It's okay, Paris. They're family."

"She worked for my dad." He kept an eye on the woman he knew as Gail and the second woman who dismounted the bike, another shifter, he guessed, given her golden eyes and the way she moved. Some sort of canine, the power in her actions more blunt, more restrained than Gail's feline power and grace.

"No," Mac said. "She works with us and is a big reason you're still alive. She helped find you that night."

Paris didn't have to ask what night he was referring to.

"I was also on that list you gave him," Gail said as she

and the other shifter approached. "You must not think I'm all bad."

"You didn't seem to want to kill me on the daily like Roni." The vampire who'd been his other keeper barely tolerated him, regularly threatening to rip his throat out with her fangs.

"She was terrible. She's also dead." Gail held out a hand to him. "Real name's Abigail."

Paris returned the shake. "Thank you for helping me."

"I wish I could have stopped him from turning you over at all."

"He didn't give you much choice, and if you had, your cover would've been blown. I get it."

"What are we doing out here?" the other shifter asked.

Abigail threw an arm over the blond's shoulders. "This is my girlfriend, Jenn. Excuse her crankiness. It runs in her family."

Jenn swatted her stomach, then turned her attention back to Mac, brow raised, expecting an answer to her earlier question. "Well . . ."

"We're looking for a giant's altar," Mac answered.

Faster than Paris could blink, Jenn spun out from under her girlfriend's arm and hauled ass back across the road toward the bike. "That's a nope."

Abigail flexed all that speed and grace Paris had witnessed on occasion, beating Jenn back to the bike and snatching the helmet out of her hands. "Did you never wonder why I left my pack? Why I came home with you from the bar that night and never left? Why I volunteered for the Cirillo gig?"

The longing in her voice, the sorrow in her dark eyes, made Paris's gut clench. Then his eyes widened and his breath stuttered as he realized what he was sensing, the sadness and loss in her aura—purple and indigo, black around the edges—but a center of pure green that anchored her to this place.

To Nature.

"Babe," Jenn said, likewise sensing her girlfriend's distress. She slid the helmet from her grasp, set it back on the bike, then curled an arm around her.

"One of the giants infiltrated our pack," Abigail told them. "Manipulated them into doing his and Chaos's bidding. Helping him hunt. I couldn't stay."

"And my father," Paris said, "had connections to a giant."

Abigail nodded. "At least one. Maybe the others. Maybe the one who turned my pack against who and what we are. I was determined to find out who he was. This is my fight too."

Paris approached cautiously, sensing Jenn on the protective edge and not fully trusting him yet. Fair. He raised his hands, palms out, then slowly stretched one out toward Abigail. She placed her hand in his, and he gave it a gentle squeeze. "Thank you again."

She squeezed back, the green in her aura pulsing brighter, then, swapping his hand for Jenn's, turned toward the woods. "Let's go. I know where the altar is."

Paris shouldered his backpack, stepped to the edge of the woods, then paused. "Um, as the only human here, I have to ask . . . Should we be worried about being attacked?"

"We've got sentries," Mac said, pointing at the corvids overhead.

"And I don't feel them here," Abigail said. "They hunt with him. They must be out of range."

Except five minutes into their trek, Paris started to hear voices. In his head. Beside him, Mac's back snapped straight and he tilted his head, an ear to the woods. "You hear that too?" Paris asked him.

He glanced over, eyes violet, and nodded. Above them, Liam croaked a plaintive call; even he sensed something amiss. Mac flashed him a two-fingered gesture, and the raven went scouting ahead. "He'll check it out," Mac said, moving closer as they followed Abigail deeper into the woods.

The voices getting louder with each step.

If he closed his eyes and opened his mind the way he had with Mac in front of the mural that day, the way the witches had been teaching him, Paris was sure he'd land in a world of violet the same color as Mac's eyes.

He reached out and tangled his fingers with Mac's, giving them a squeeze to get his attention. *Are you sure she's on our side?* he mouthed, asking a question he knew the answer to but hoped he was wrong.

Mac didn't hesitate to nod, and Paris swallowed hard, dreading what the voices meant, what they were going to find at the altar. Even more certain of it when Liam came sailing back through the woods to perch on Mac's shoulder, his glossy black head bowed.

A scout was no longer needed; a reaper was.

"Abigail," Mac called. "Why don't you let us go ahead?"

She spun on her heel, asking "Why?" at the same time Jenn said, "I smell smoke."

Abigail sniffed the air once, and then she was off and running, Jenn on her heels, Liam darting after them.

"Fucking coyotes," Mac said, shoving a hand through his hair. "Zero tact."

"They're dead, aren't they?" Paris said. "Abigail's pack? That's who I'm hearing."

Mac dropped his arm, then his shoulders, and all of him looked tired already. Answer enough. "Let's get you back to the car," he said. "I'll send Liam back to drive you to the cabin. I'm going to be here a while."

Paris lowered his bag and withdrew the canteen of water, taking a slug as he debated how to ask what he wanted and get the answer he wanted too. Because contrary to what he was sure Mac was going to say, he wasn't taking no for an answer. "You can help them? Even if they're not on your list?"

He offered the bottle to Mac who took a longer swallow. "It's harder to make the connection, but it's doable. I have to try. Their souls deserve peace."

"Can I help make that connection?" He took the bottle back from Mac and tucked it in the bag. "Direct the souls your way?"

"Paris, I can't ask—"

"You're not asking." An even better approach. "I can help you, and I can maybe learn more about what happened to me and the giants' plans. This is my fight too," he said, repeating Abigail's words. He shouldered his bag and started moving again, the way Abigail and Jenn had disappeared. "Let's go."

Mac drew even with him but didn't try to stop his forward momentum. "This isn't going to be pretty."

"I know. I lived through it."

Famous last words.

Smoke was thankfully all that lingered in the air, the magical fire having reduced everything to ash, but the utter devastation had Paris falling to his knees. He hadn't been there to witness the aftermath of his own near death, and destruction was par for the course in the Canyon Lands, but the black hole that dark magic had left here—in a place of otherworldly beauty, the altar in a meadow like the one near the cabin, its view of the sky unobstructed and above the fog line—took his breath away.

And on the heels of that blow came the one in his head, all of the voices crashing into him at once, a cacophony like the one that had assaulted him on the altar in YB.

"Breathe, Paris." Mac's hand on his nape, the tug in his chest, quieted the souls a measure. "Breathe through it, tell them to hold on while I check on Abigail, and then we'll get to work. But wait for me, okay?"

Paris nodded, not about to undertake this without an anchor, not even about to argue when Mac made a flicking motion with his hand, and Liam flitted down onto Paris's shoulder. He needed the backup, but Abigail needed Mac more at the moment. "Go, I'll wait."

As he did, he tried to ignore the horror and survey the scene, like Mac the investigator would, having observed him walk through his murals the same way. The higher mound of ash that was likely where the altar had been, the smaller mounds that dotted the clearing in a semicircle, witnesses to the monster's sacrifice. Questions roiled in Paris's head along with the voices.

What had this giant done to sway these shifters to his side?

Had he died in the blast too, or was he still out there?

Were any of the pack?

Who was the human sacrifice? How many others had been sacrificed on the altar? How much power had Chaos gained as a result? How much trouble were they truly in?

THIRTEEN

BY THE TIME Mac left to ferry the last soul, the sky was full of stars above. Paris wondered again if one of those bright, twinkling lights was his mother, if she'd heard his plea to take good care of the innocents Mac had delivered today.

And there had been innocents, more than a few. Pack children who hadn't chosen Chaos, other members of the pack who'd been held against their will, the human—Dylan—who had been hunted in these woods for days. He'd been lured here by his best friend, a mountain lion from the pack. Paris had lost his breath when he'd first delved into his memories, nearly drowning from the tidal wave of betrayal Dylan had felt. He couldn't imagine Kai or Jason ever doing such a thing, but Dylan hadn't imagined his best friend would either. They'd been closer than blood, but then his friend's blind allegiance to Chaos, his fear of Nature's evolving world, had turned him against Dylan. Through Dylan's unbelieving human eyes, Paris had watched as his friend had stood next to the giant by the altar and, with his own claws, torn Dylan's heart from his chest. As Dylan's last breath escaped, as the bond he'd shared with his friend well and truly severed, the giant had lost control of the magic and burned everything and everyone to the ground. Paris didn't think the timing was a coincidence.

Nor did he think it a coincidence that Mac's violet eyes were dim and his flying off-kilter when he eventually returned. Liam took up position on his wing and guided him to Paris's shoulder. He landed, and it was like a blast chiller flipping on beside Paris, frigid air blanketing his cheek. The raven was shivering too, cold all the way to his talons. Paris needed to get him back to the cabin, ASAP.

Kneeling, he dug two sets of clothes out of his pack, placing the jeans and sweater on the ground next to Liam and the extra sweats in a pile for Mac. He'd intended them for himself, but Mac needed them more right now. "Shift and change," he told the giant black bird on his shoulder. "I'll tell Jenn and Abigail we're finished."

It was a testament to Mac's exhaustion that he didn't argue, that he simply hopped off Paris's shoulder and onto the pile of jersey material without protest. Paris crossed the large singed circle to where Jenn stood sentry over Abigail, who was scooping ashes into bowls they'd fashioned from pieces of tree bark outside the burn zone.

"I need to get Mac back to the cabin."

Abigail twisted to glance up at him. "Are all the souls gone?"

Paris nodded, suddenly feeling the weight of exhaustion in his own bones, in his head that had been a virtual drive-thru the past twelve hours as they'd sorted who and which direction souls would travel, what each soul deserved. "That's all of them."

"I couldn't feel them," Abigail said as she stood. "But you and Mac and Liam could." She handed the bowl to Jenn then pulled him into her arms. "Thank you."

He hugged her back. "Thank you for keeping me alive all those months. And we will catch the giant who did this to your people." He had a mural to paint, as soon as he got back to the cabin and got Mac buried under a mountain of blankets. "You're good here?" he asked. "Safe?"

"I can stay," Liam said, rejoining them in human form.

Jenn shook her head. "You need to rest too, but you also need to get this one"—she tilted her head toward Paris—"and Mac back down the mountain in one piece. Leave the rest of the birds. We'll text when we get home."

Paris was still learning about the team Mac spoke of often, still sorting out the hierarchy, but he surmised Adam was at the top and Jenn close by, given how easily she issued orders and how quickly Liam acquiesced. She was all business. Was she the *her* they spoke of? In any event, Paris was caught off guard when the gruff leader likewise drew him into a hug. "Thank you for doing this for her." The embrace was stiff and awkward but the words sincere, and despite the awful day, Paris couldn't hide his smile. He liked Abigail a lot, and Jenn clearly loved her and would do anything for her.

The coyote had another message for him. "Adam needs Mac," she said. "And she's not done with him yet either. We're trusting you."

So *she* wasn't Jenn, and Paris didn't think Jenn was referring to Abigail either. Nor did he think he'd ever been trusted with something so important. It scared him but also filled him with pride, something that had been in short supply during his relatively short life. He intended to keep earning it.

"I've got him."

———

"What do you need?" Mac asked, even as Paris, shoulder under his, hauled him through the cabin door.

Between the full-body shivers, chattering teeth, and cold, clammy skin, Mac had deteriorated more with each passing mile on the drive back to the cabin. Concern for him at fever pitch, Paris guided the raven across the room and lowered him onto the end of the bed. "I need you to lie down and go to sleep."

"Paris—"

"And leave your clothes on," he ordered, borrowing some of Jenn's authority. "You're freezing."

"It's normal."

"I don't think it is." He held up the sheets and blankets for Mac. "You're overworked, like you were that morning after guiding Icarus and Adam."

"He's not wrong," Liam said as he closed the cabin door behind them. "About any of it. Go to sleep, brother. I'll keep an eye on Paris."

Mac's answering glare gave Paris a measure of comfort, as did his acquiescence, the exhausted reaper finally crawling under the covers. By the time Paris was back with another blanket to throw over him, he was snoring. With Mac tucked in and warm, Paris closed his eyes to recenter himself, breathing in the scents of life in the cabin—the vases full of wildflowers, the bread he'd made yesterday, the lingering scent of fresh paint.

"You should sleep too," Liam said from where he was crouched in front of the fire, stoking it back to life.

Paris righted his head and flexed his fingers. "I need to paint while the giant is fresh in my head. I don't want to forget any details." This giant looked nothing like the one who'd taken him. He was big, bulky, and bald, and there were more things to distinguish him. Hazel eyes that weren't quite the same size, eyelashes so thick they looked kohl-lined, a birthmark in front of one ear, a tattoo inside one wrist.

He grabbed his paints and brushes and the wooden platter he'd repurposed as a palette and stood in front of the freshly repainted wall, close to the light of the fire.

Liam appeared at his side a couple minutes later. "Here," he said, offering Paris a mug of steaming tea. "For your stomach. I know that drive wasn't easy on you." Liam, bless him, had sped down the mountain so fast Paris's stomach was left somewhere back there on the winding road.

"I wouldn't have told you to slow down, no matter how sick I felt."

"I know." He glanced Mac's direction as he lowered onto the couch, the concern in his gaze the same that thrummed through Paris. "Thank you for that and for helping him. He couldn't have done that today without you."

"Or without you."

"I wish he'd let me do more."

"I know," Paris said, parroting Liam's earlier response. He swiped his brush through the brown and green paint and started the mural with the giant's eyes. "Your aura is pure indigo. Empathy, according to the witches."

"You can read auras?" Back to Liam, Paris couldn't see his eyes, but by the tone of his voice, he bet they were wide.

"It started with Mac's, then today I could see Abigail's, and now yours. I've been working with the witches to understand what I'm seeing. Still not sure on the who or the why yet."

He worked more on the outline of the giant's face—a larger than average forehead, a square, clean-shaven jaw, a crooked nose that had been broken multiple times. The silence was comfortable, Liam's presence familiar, but conversation helped keep the fear at bay. "Can there be two reapers at once?" Paris asked.

"Everyone in our family can sense the souls."

Paris glanced over his shoulder. "About five minutes into the trek, I started hearing the voices and a split second later, you *Kraa*'ed." His attempt to mimic their call drew a welcome chuckle out of Liam.

"I heard them too," he said, but then sobered, gaze straying again to where Mac was curled on his side in bed. "We can all sense them because both our parents were reapers. Our mother was the reaper for her tribe, our father from his Celtic ancestors' clan, but when they mated, the lines were joined, and there can only be one reaper from a line who crosses between the planes. I watch and learn and do what I can to help on this one whenever he'll let me."

"It'll be you next?" Paris asked as he turned back to the wall.

"If he doesn't outlive me."

"He can't give it up?"

"He can. Our parents did. But he won't."

Paris wasn't sure that was quite right. Not with the

regret and duty that colored so much of Mac's aura. "Or he doesn't know how."

Liam hummed in reply, contemplating it seemed. His silence stretched on so long that Paris assumed he'd fallen asleep, until the couch cushions squeaked again sometime later, Liam rising to stoke the fire. "Is he okay?"

"He's exhausted—and exhausting," Paris said with a smile as he tinkered with the almost leaf-like collection of freckles behind the giant's ear. "But I don't think he knows any other way to be." Liam's answering laugh was warm and affectionate. "Am I wrong?"

"You're not, but he's different with you. Since you."

"If I can use that to make him sleep, then let's count it a win."

"It's going to get tougher," Liam said as he stood beside Paris in front of the wall. "Especially with the Rift anniversary in a few days. I need you—*we* need you—to keep helping him. He lets you, more than he lets any of us." The urgency in his voice made Paris pause mid-brushstroke and glance in his direction. And was nearly blinded by the pure indigo aura that radiated out of him. "Keep making him sleep. Make him talk too, when he needs that. Too many people, too many souls depend on him."

Paris nodded, for all their sakes and his own, because if the tugging in his chest today each time he dove into a vision, each time Mac came and went between the planes was any indication, Paris's soul depended on Mac too.

FOURTEEN

PARIS SURRENDERED his brush at sunrise, every detail he could muster about the giant out of his head and onto the wall. Mind and body tired, all he wanted to do was shut his eyes and forget the world for a while. He stoked the fire, made sure Liam's blankets were snug around him on the couch, then crawled into bed with a relieved sigh.

Only for worry to spike when Mac's shivers rippled across the mattress. Not as severe as earlier, and for a good long while there, he'd slept peacefully, but Paris didn't like that the tremors were back. He considered more covers, but all of them in the cabin were already in use, and he sure as hell wasn't going for a walk in the morning cold to fetch one from the witches. Taking the only action left to him, Paris scooted closer and spooned the taller man from behind. Mac didn't wake, didn't even move but for the tremors that continued to ripple through his body. Paris held him close and distracted himself from the mounting worry by counting Liam's snores from across the room. Fifty-six later, Mac's shivers finally subsided, his breaths evening out again, and before Paris reached sixty, he nodded off himself, forehead pressed against the soft fabric between Mac's shoulder blades.

When he woke sometime later, Paris detected no snores, no voices, and no keystrokes, just the sizzling crackle of a waning fire. Opening his eyes, Paris let them adjust to the dim lighting, the late afternoon sun cutting across the cabin. And catching the note on the pillow beside his. Unfolding it, he recognized Mac's handwriting from his case files. *Thank you*, it read. *We're needed in YB. Coven is here for anything you need. Back soon. —M*

Two days later, Paris was raring for an argument over the definition of soon, if soon ever came to pass. There'd been no sign of Mac or Liam, no word from any of Paris's own contacts in YB, and no calls that the witches told him about during their lessons or over the dinner Paris made for them last night. While Paris appreciated Mac's trust in leaving him out here alone, while he appreciated the peace and protection of this forest by the sea, not knowing what was going on outside it, not knowing if he could help like he had on the ridge, was driving him crazy. The only things that kept him sane, that kept him from hot-wiring one of the witch's cars like Jason had taught him, were his paints and the unwavering connection he shared with Mac. Mac was out there, doing what his team needed, and the last thing he needed was Paris distracting him. He'd all but resigned himself to not seeing Mac or Liam until after the Rift anniversary tomorrow, so when tires crunched over the gravel outside, he nearly dropped his paintbrush.

Righting his grip on the brush, he flipped it so the pointy end was at the ready. Mac had told him only friend-lies could get through the witches' protections and the crows in the trees. He wasn't expecting any witchy visitors, so . . . He moved to peek out the window, but before he reached it, the door swung open, Mac's tall, rangy frame stepping through, his face shadowed by the setting sun outside.

Paris opened his mouth to have that argument about *soon*, but then the light shifted and Mac's face came into full view. His tan skin was pale, dark circles underlined his eyes, and his hair was a tousled mess. Add the slumped shoulders under his wrinkled shirt and the tie hanging loose around his neck, and Paris didn't want to know the last time Mac had slept. In his arms two days ago, if Paris had to guess. At least he wasn't shivering this time. In any event, he was here now, and Paris needed to get him fed and to bed.

"How about some potato fennel soup and cheese sandwiches?"

"That sounds great."

"Go take a shower while I get it ready."

Mac didn't argue, just grabbed fresh clothes from the pile Paris had cleaned and headed for the bathroom. By the time he reappeared, Paris had bowls of soup on the table and was cutting the hearth-grilled sandwiches in half.

And nearly sawed his finger in half too.

Barefoot and hair wet, Mac crossed the room in his low-slung pants and unbuttoned dress shirt, more of that long, lean body on display than Paris had ever seen. And more striking than he'd ever dreamed. He took a moment to appreciate the rosy warmth the shower had returned to his skin, then took a longer few moments to appreciate Mac's broad shoulders and solid chest, abs that were toned but not overly ripped, the sprinkling of dark curls on his torso and the thicker line of dark hairs that trailed beneath his waistband.

Paris's mouth went dry, the inevitable supernova finally crashing into him and his dick responding in kind, hardening inside his sweats. Thank fuck he was standing behind a counter where Mac couldn't see.

"I'm sorry I couldn't send word," the raven said, and Paris struggled to focus on his words and not the tempting figure he cut in the firelight. "I meant to make it back last night, but then one of the names on your list flipped, and he led us to one of your father's stash houses."

Mention of Vincent quelled Paris's libido, for now. He finished slicing the sandwiches without injury and carried the plates to the table. "What does that mean?" he asked as he and Mac took their seats.

"Money, weapons, magical beings he used as power sources."

"Alive?"

He stirred his soup, a faraway look flitting across his dark eyes. "Some."

"But not as bad as the ridge?" Paris said, if he was reading the reaper's vitals correctly. "You weren't shivering when you came in."

Mac returned to the present and his food, slurping a spoonful of still steaming soup. Paris was glad he'd leaned toward over-warm. "No, thankfully, and we had another reaper helping."

"I wish I could've been there to help you."

"Me too." He aimed one of his soft smiles in Paris's direction, and Paris flip-flopped again on which expression to paint. He had time to decide, the rest of the picture still coming together in his head, the rest of the world still on fire. He wanted to paint Mac when it wasn't a necessity; when instead it was simply a matter of joy and appreciation.

They finished their soup and sandwiches in silence, jazz music playing in the background, and when Paris rose and carried the dishes to the sink, Mac joined him. "We took the physical weapons," he said. "But the money is yours. We've secured it."

"Use what you need for Nature's cause."

"Paris."

He flung a soapy hand in the air, gesturing at their surroundings. "How much have you spent on paints, on clothes, on food, on taking care of me?"

"That's not even a blip on the radar of what you've inherited."

Paris gulped. He'd known his father—their family—was rich, but he'd purposely looked the other way, ignored the how and why and stayed in his privileged golden cage. No more. "I don't want that money."

"If you don't claim it, someone else will, and not for good."

"Fine," he gritted out, fists balled under the soapy water. "Use what you need for the cause, then I'll find more good uses for the rest. Deal?"

"Deal." Mac bumped his shoulder and warmth rippled out from the simple contact, easing Paris back down from his momentary fuss. Unclenching his fists, he got back to washing dishes, and Mac grabbed the closest dishtowel to dry. "Dinner was delicious," he said.

"The witches have been good to me." Checking up on him, teaching him about auras, joining him in the meadow to pick flowers and other herbs they'd discovered among the weeds. "I wanted to do something nice for them. More than just regular bread deliveries."

Mac gifted him another soft smile, then, once they were finished, wandered out of the kitchen area. "You stayed painting while I was gone. They're so bright," he said from in front of the wall of flowers bursting with color, pretty things his father would never let him have. Belittled him for painting. "You left this, though," Mac said with a nod toward the mural of the giant from the ridge.

"I didn't know if you had enough light or enough time to take a picture before you left."

"I did, and we got a positive ID on him."

Pride swelled inside Paris's chest. He'd done something right, had turned the worst moment of his life into some-thing good, into something he could use to help Mac and the team. He'd been told his entire life he was a fool, that he was worthless, but in this case he'd remembered enough, painted well enough to give Mac a lead. Maybe Icarus had been right when he'd told Paris not to sell himself short. "Have you found him yet?"

"Not yet, but Icarus's sister is digging into his financials and internet history. We're trying to pinpoint where he might set up for Samhain."

"One of the other altars?"

"That's the thinking, but we have to find them first."

"Are there other thin spots like the one on the ridge?"

"More than a few," Mac answered. "But we don't have an insider like we did with Abigail and the last one. We'll have to approach the rest with caution." He gestured again at the wall. "Let's paint over this one."

"In the morning," Paris replied. "You need to go to bed."

"I do," he conceded. "But if I have any hope of sleeping, I need to get out of my head first. Mindlessly rolling paint onto a wall should do the trick."

"Fair enough," Paris said with a chuckle. "You get the paint ready. I'm going to turn up the music and swap these sweats for the paint-stained ones."

A quick trip to the bathroom, then Paris returned just as one of his favorite tunes began to fill the cabin, its cresting and breaking melodies reminding him of the waves he'd gone too many days without again.

The ocean . . .

"Wait!" he called out to Mac who was running the roller brush through the tray of white paint. Mac paused, gaze straying over his shoulder. "I want to start from a different base color," Paris explained. He snagged his tubes of blue and indigo and added several dollops of the former and a single dollop of the latter to the tray. He swirled them into the white, mixing the colors, but it still wasn't quite the shade in his head. He snatched his tube of green off the nearby table, added a dollop of that too, and after several more stirs, the tray of paint finally transformed into the lovely blue-green shade he missed so much.

"The ocean," Mac said, catching on.

"Not just the shore this time." Grinning, Paris made a giant sweeping gesture. "I want a whole wall of ocean."

Mac's answering laugh was worth the dramatics.

Paris grabbed the other roller, and they worked together to cover the nightmare mural with cool blue-green, the rhythmic roll of the brushes, the smooth jazz notes filling the cabin, and the crackling fire creating the cocoon of calm they'd both needed. Paris might even go so far as to say an uplift in Mac's mood, the typically restrained raven swaying his hips to the tune as he ran the roller through the paint tray again. "He dances," Paris gasped, playing dramatic again, hoping for a similar reaction.

Mac rolled his eyes and swiped at the hair that had fallen across his forehead. "He sways because he can barely stay upright."

"I don't believe you." Leaving his roller propped against the wall, Paris gently removed Mac's from his hand and rested it beside his, then just as gently drew Mac by the wrist into his arms.

Around a smile, Mac grumbled, "What are you doing?"

"Dancing." And taking his chance, Mac's walls and defenses down, his limbs loose and body warm. Paris shifted closer, soaking up the energy that vibrated between them.

"Paris," Mac whispered, voice trembling. "I can't—"

Yes, you can was on the tip of his tongue, but when Paris looked into Mac's eyes, when he saw the desire and terror swirling in the dark depths, he altered course, desperate not to drive whatever had put that fear in his gaze higher. That was the last thing Mac needed. He laid a hand on Mac's chest and ignored his own desire to drag his fingers through the curls there. "I'm not asking for anything, Mac. Just dancing with a friend and helping you get out of your head."

The sound that slipped from Mac's lips was somewhere between a laugh and a groan, and he tilted forward, forehead pressed against Paris's. "You're doing more than that." He cupped the side of Paris's neck, and Paris's heart leapt. Jumped all the way into his throat as Mac angled his face, breath coasting over his lips.

And then gone the next instant, and it took Paris a

disorienting second to realize why. Someone was banging on the cabin door, and every muscle in Mac's frame had snapped tight, gone battle-ready, his gaze fixed on the door.

"It's probably just Liam or one of the witches," Paris said, even as his own pulse raced faster, adrenaline kicking in to help him fight or flee.

"If it was Liam, I would have sensed him. And the witches know to signal." He stepped out of Paris's arms and peeked out the side window into the trees. "Why didn't the crows alert me?"

Had someone found them? Someone who wanted to kidnap him for his inheritance? Or someone who worked for Chaos? Was it the giant coming back for him? "Mac . . ." he whispered, his voice trembling now.

Mac grabbed the bread knife off the counter and slapped the handle into Paris's hand. "Take this and go hide in the bathroom."

"*What?*"

"Paris, *please.*" When he lifted his gaze, his eyes were glowing violet, all trace of desire gone, nothing but terror now. He had no idea who was on the other side of that door, and he feared the worst. Paris grabbed hold of that imaginary rope inside his chest and tugged. Mac tugged right back. "Go."

FIFTEEN

WHEN A MINUTE PASSED without the pop of gunfire or the crack of furniture, Paris nudged open the bathroom door. Hearing no raised voices or other sounds of a fight, he opened the door wider and peeked out. Mac was standing over the front door threshold, puffed up and growly, blocking Paris's view of their visitor and their visitor's view of him. He fed his crush that protective nugget, wallowing in it, until his name—"Paris Cirillo"—reached his ears.

"I don't know who you're talking about," Mac lied.

"I know he's here," said the voice Paris would recognize anywhere. Out of any danger, Paris set aside his makeshift weapons and hustled across the cabin.

"How's that?" Mac practically barked.

"Because I told him," Paris said, talking over his best friend's "Because I can smell him." Strange reply, but whatever . . . Kai was *here*. Paris ducked under Mac's arm and swallowed the smaller man in a crushing hug.

"You *what*?" Mac barked at him now, and Paris would get to that truth in just a moment.

For now, he wanted to revel in the familiar, in his first taste of home in over a week, and it warmed his heart that Kai hugged him back just as fiercely. The three of them—Kai, Jason, and Paris—were family, the real kind, and Paris had missed them, dearly. He drew back, checking his friend over, from his dark tousled curls to his tan skin to his big brown eyes. "I missed you," Paris said to him, then glancing over his shoulder at a simmering Mac, color high in his cheeks, fingers white-knuckling the door, added, "He's a friend. One of my best."

"No one is supposed to know you're here," Mac said, voice strained. "Not after the last time."

Okay, he had a point, and a right to be angry—no contact was one of the rules—but if it had been a hard and fast one, Liam wouldn't have let him use his phone that day. And Paris's position from that day hadn't changed. He wasn't going to leave his human friends stranded in the middle of a magical shitstorm without some kind of backup.

Was that why Kai was here now? Were he and Jason in trouble? Where was Jason? All questions he wanted answers to—inside the cabin. "It's fine," he told Mac. "We can trust him." He shifted from Kai's arms to Mac's side and patted his chest, seeking to assure the raven in the same place Paris felt his reassurance whenever he needed it. "Now, can we let him in before the witches get even more curious? The crows are audience enough."

With a combination glare and growl that would turn Paris on at any other time, Mac begrudgingly opened the door wide enough for Paris to slip back through with Kai in tow.

"What are you doing here?" he asked as Kai glanced around the cabin.

Mac closed the door, then stood beside them, arms crossed. "Better question. Why didn't the crows alert me that you were here in the first place?"

Kai shifted Paris's grip, flipping it so he was the one squeezing Paris's hand. The apology in his eyes nearly startled a gasp out of Paris. "You gotta promise not to be mad at me. This wasn't about you."

Not about him? Mad at Kai? For what? Showing up here? Not possible. "I missed you too much to be mad."

Kai released his hand, then held his own out to Mac. "Because I'm one of you. Kai Finley."

Paris did gasp at that. One of you, as in a raven? A shifter?

Eyes wide, Mac seemed as surprised as him for once. "What's your real name?"

"Kaimus. Finley was my father's surname. My mother's was Kasta."

"Haida?" Mac asked, and Kai nodded. When Mac spoke again, his tone did a complete one-eighty from suspicious to almost . . . reverent. "I thought your kind were gone."

His kind? So he wasn't a raven? And what was Haida? Kai rarely spoke about his parents or where he'd come from before landing in YB, but he had mentioned his mother was from an Indigenous tribe up north. Was Haida that tribe? Of shifters?

"Not gone," Kai said. "Just hiding."

"Cormac Kelley. It's an honor. And please, call me Mac."

Head spinning, Paris slid between the two men,

glancing back and forth between them. "I'm lost. Can someone please explain?"

"You didn't know he was a raven?" Mac said.

"Clearly." He pointed at Kai's face. "And his eyes are brown." Only humans had brown eyes.

"Not really," Kai said, apology in his gaze once more. Standing beside the table, he removed a case from his pocket and removed contacts Paris had never suspected, had never seen him put in or take out before. When Kai lifted his gaze back to them, his blue-green irises were again not what Paris expected.

"They're not purple like yours," he said to Mac.

"No, because he's a different kind of raven. He's special, Paris."

"Well, the *special* part I knew." Kai was the best of them, the one who'd gone straight and earned an honest living tending bar. He was calm, he was caring, he kept him and Jason in line as much as he could. Paris trusted him completely, but not the other way around, it seemed? He couldn't keep the hurt from his voice. "But the other . . ."

Kai captured his flailing hand. "I'm sorry. With your dad, I couldn't risk him finding out what I was."

"Does anyone in YB know?" Mac asked.

"Our other best friend, Jason. He's the only person here I've told."

That stung, not because Kai hadn't told him, but because Paris's father had stolen something else from him, had put a wall between Paris and his best friends. One of whom was conspicuously absent, and with everything Paris had learned about ravens lately, Paris's worry ratcheted higher. "Where is he?"

"That's why I'm here. I think he's in trouble." He shifted his gaze to Mac. "The raven knows he is."

"Jason's always in trouble," Paris said, though he sensed something was different this time. It had to be for Kai to risk coming here, to expose his identity. Paris squeezed his hand in solidarity, letting him know he didn't hold anything against him, that he still had his back.

Kai nodded, then turned his attention back to Mac and lifted his other hand, splaying it over his chest. "It burns."

The resemblance to the motion Paris had just shared with Mac was unmistakable. He wasn't surprised his best friends were connected in a similar way. But what did he mean by *it burns*? "What's happened?" he asked as he led them to the seating area, Mac buttoning his shirt along the way.

Kai lowered himself on one end of the couch. "Moira."

Because *of course* it would be her. Paris flopped next to Kai and hung his head back on a groan. "Fucking hell."

"Who's Moira?" Mac asked from the chair.

"Asshole vampire of the highest order." He righted his gaze and flicked a hand in the air. "She and Jason were a thing for a hot minute."

"She told him there was a stash." Kai cleared his throat and glanced guiltily at Paris. "One of your father's in the Canyon Lands. She needed a lock pick."

"And Jason needed a payday," Paris surmised.

"To get us out before tomorrow."

Paris looped an arm around Kai's shoulders and pulled him into a sideways hug. Why wouldn't his friends just let him help? Jason didn't have to put himself in danger; Kai wouldn't have to worry about him. Granted, it was more complicated when Vincent had been alive, especially if Kai hadn't wanted to expose himself, but now . . . Now, when whatever this was was all over, they were going to have a serious conversation about how to stay alive, all of them, because Paris needed his family.

"I didn't know where else to go," Kai said.

"This is why I told you where I was, in case of emergency." It gave him some hope they could work out an arrangement in the future. Now he just needed Mac's help in the present. "I'm sorry, but I needed them to have some backup."

Mac's gaze held his for a long moment, understanding passing between them, before he leaned forward and rested his forearms on his knees. "You said it burns. What did you mean?"

"That they're connected," Paris said, and barely bit back the *like us* he wanted to add. Would Mac want that shared with Kai? Did Mac feel the same way?

"There's connected," Mac said. "And then there's 'it burns.' Very different."

"You know what my people did?" Kai asked, and at Mac's nod, he continued. "I think—" He cut himself off, swallowed hard, then started again. "I *know* Jason's a phoenix. And he's in danger."

"But Jason's human," Paris said, voice rising with panic, the world starting to spin again.

"Not anymore."

Mac rested a hand on his knee. "Breathe, Paris." Squeezed. "You did the right thing. We'll try to help him." He left his hand there as he glanced back to Kai. "I need to know everything."

For all of Atlas's efforts to make sure he was well-read and educated, Paris had gotten a crash course in the supernatural the past twelve days. And as Mac and Kai talked, as Kai divulged more details, Paris tried to suppress how overwhelmed he felt and focus instead on the mundane because that was the only way he could help in this situation.

He zeroed in on certain words from their conversation.

Stash.

Phoenix.

Power.

Staring at the calming blue-green wall, the same color as his friend's real eyes, Paris put himself in the shoes of the person he had the misfortune to know best in the world.

Vincent Cirillo.

The human who had hunted phoenixes, held them captive in stash houses, and bled them dry in order to replenish his own stolen power.

Fuel stations, his father used to say. *I need to visit a fuel station.*

Fuel stations that were marked on a map he kept in his private study, a room only he and Atlas had ever been inside. That Paris regularly broke into to steal from his father's supply of Daylight.

Rocketing off the couch, he grabbed the closest paint brush and the tubes of black and red paint. He squeezed a dollop of each onto the back of his hand, swiped his brush through the black one first, then on the blue-green wall, he began to sketch the outlines of the Canyon Lands. Crumbling stone jetties and canyons of deep, dark water, broken buildings and disintegrating streets, the barbed wire fence that separated what amounted to YB's haunted house from the rest of the city.

He was so deep in his memories, so focused on translating them correctly onto the wall, that he didn't notice the conversation behind him quiet or Mac move to stand behind him. He startled when he rocked back on one heel to evaluate his work and ran into him.

"What's this?" Mac asked, steadying him by the shoulders.

"My father had maps. Lots of them." He rinsed his brush in the paint water mug, flicked off the excess, then swiped it through the red. "There was this one in his private office. It had red dots on it." He marked the five spots on the map he'd replicated. "When I asked him what the dots were, he told me they were fuel stations."

Mac stepped beside him, stared a long moment at the wall, and then a satisfied smirk stretched across his face, the sexiest thing Paris had ever seen. "You're amazing," he said, clasping the back of Paris's head and hauling it closer to press his lips to his temple, searing Paris with the affectionate touch. "Go pack."

Wait . . . what? Paris jerked his head back, meeting the raven's dark eyes. "We're leaving?"

"I need to go into the city with Kai, but I'll send Liam for you. If your friend is a phoenix, if he survives, we'll need to bring him back to the mountain after. I assume you'll want to be with him."

"Yes, of course," Paris said as he tossed aside his brush and wiped his hands on his sweats. "But why are we going back to the ridge?"

"Not the ridge," Mac said. "We're going to Monte Corvo. In Talahalusi."

SIXTEEN

LIAM TURNED off Talahalusi's main road and onto a paved drive blocked by iron gates, each adorned with a giant raven, their wings spread wide, and in the middle where the gates met, the letters MC molded in ornate script.

"Not hiding, are you?" Paris said.

"It was called Crow Mountain before our mother's people settled it." Liam reached out the window and pressed his thumb to a keypad. "No matter the language, that's what it means." The gates swung open, and Liam drove through. "In the light of day, you'll understand why."

In the light of the car's high beams, Paris counted row after row of vines as the road snaked higher. Around one bend, a pair of long barn-like facilities appeared on either side of the road, stretching as far as Paris could see in the dark. Around the next one, a massive mansion—correction, castle—stood majestically on a clearing.

But they weren't done climbing yet. Liam circled behind the castle and veered off the paved road onto a gravel one, and up, up, up they went, all the way to where the vegetation and trees thinned out and a smaller version of the mansion below set atop the bluff. "This is the reaper's perch," Liam said as he parked in front of the stone steps that led to the front door.

Paris climbed out of the car and wandered to the edge of the bluff. Nothing but darkness below and starlight above. He rotated back to Liam and gestured at the relatively miniature castle. "If Mac lives in this monster, who lives in the bigger one down the hill?" The Cirillos were rich by YB standards, but the kind of wealth that built these structures, that cultivated this land was generational, far eclipsing Paris's father's ill-gotten gains. Hell, the real estate value alone dwarfed their compound of penthouse condos.

Liam chuckled. "Me and the rest of the family."

"Are you sure they're not all here?" Every light in Mac's place was on, several other cars were parked in the circular drive, and music played from somewhere inside.

"This is also the team's main base of operations." Starting for the front door, his foot had barely hit the bottom step when the door swung open and two children came screaming through, yelling "Daddy!" at the top of their lungs.

"Daddy?" Paris squawked.

"Not that kind," Liam said with a wink over his shoulder before he kneeled with his arms open for . . . his kids? "Hello, my tiny terrors."

They barreled into him, all giggles, and Liam laughed along with them, that full-bellied one Paris had heard before. Now he understood where Liam's wealth of happiness came from—these two children with the same sharp Kelley nose and black eyes, with skin that was several shades darker, and with brown hair that was coarse and curly. Close in age, if Paris had to guess, around five or six, and the both of them chatty, talking over each other as they told their father what all they'd been up to. Paris caught Icarus's name several times, the mention of crocheting, and then as fast as they'd appeared, the siblings raced back inside.

Standing, Liam wiped the gravel off his knees, and without the cute distracting chatterboxes, Paris's confusion retook center stage. "I had no idea you were a dad. Do you single parent, or do you have a partner?"

"That would be me," came a new voice from the doorway, and Paris swung his gaze her direction. Tall, curvy, with dark skin, black eyes, and brown hair, and ripped biceps that gave away the fact she could probably kick both his and Liam's asses.

That knowledge, unfortunately, did not reach Paris's mouth before he said to Liam, "But you flirt with—"

"Everyone," Liam's partner said, her smile belying her beleaguered groan. She sashayed down the steps, hands in the pockets of her patterned dress. "Thankfully, I married him first."

"Because you've known since we were toddlers that I was yours." He held out an arm, and the woman slid under it, nestled against his side. "Paris, my wife, Rena. Rena, this is Paris."

"And those rug rats are our kids," Rena said. "Cherry and Abernathy."

Paris raised a brow, the contrast between the names stark.

"We let them choose," Liam said. "And after some back-and-forth, that's where we've landed."

"For now," Rena said, and by her tone, Paris fully expected the kids to have different names by tomorrow. Their prerogative.

"I'm sorry I've kept Liam away from you all lately," Paris said as he followed the happy couple inside.

"My parents are winemakers," Rena explained. "They came here to run the blending operation when I was a baby. I grew up with this one." She elbowed Liam's side. "I knew what I was signing up for."

Liam hugged her close and plastered a sloppy, wet kiss on her cheek that they all laughed over. "The kids should be asleep," he said as he drew back.

"You tell that to Icarus when he gets back. He bet them a cupcake each they couldn't out-stitch him. Pretty sure he let them win."

"That sounds like Icarus," Paris said, the vampire one of the more mischievous beings he'd ever met. But he was also inherently good-natured; of course he'd let the kids beat him.

"You know him?" Rena asked.

"Quite well," he replied, heat hitting his cheeks. Impossible for it not to given the very mischievous things, usually involving lace and blindfolds, he and Icarus had gotten up to since the courtesan had arrived in town nine months ago.

"Uh-oh," Rena said, brow lifted. "Are we going to have to referee a match between him and Adam?" she asked Liam.

Paris opened his mouth to reply, but Liam beat him to it. "No, honey, he's bonded to Mac."

Her assessing gaze shot back to him, even as she directed her question at Liam. "That's still possible? After—"

"Apparently."

Paris shook his head, losing the thread back around the word *bond*. "I'm sorry, what—"

Before he could finish his question, Cherry and Abernathy came racing back toward them, each waving what looked like pot holders at Liam. "Dad! Look it!"

"Amazing!" Liam oohed and aahed like a good parent should, until Rena eventually nipped the too late party in the bud. "We need to get them home and to bed."

The kids booed, but Liam gamely lifted one on each hip, advising, "Your mom is the smartest person on Earth. We have to do what she says. She's always right."

"I thought that was Mary," Abernathy said.

"Smartest," Liam said. "Mary's the most powerful."

Mary? Who was that? Paris was lost again.

"Can you show him to Mac's quarters?" Liam said to Rena, then said to Paris, "I'll be back to unpack once I get them to sleep."

Paris shook his head and held out his hand. "Give me the keys and I'll take care of it." He counted it a win that Liam didn't hesitate.

"Are Monte and Chaz here?" Liam asked Rena as he kissed her cheek once more.

"Down by the lake preparing for containment. Two of the coyotes are on guard."

"Good," Liam said with a nod, then readjusted the kids on his hips and shot Paris a smile. "Make yourself at home."

Once Liam carried the children out the front door, Rena closed it behind him, then waved Paris deeper into the house. "There's a lake here?" he asked, and they made conversation while he stared agape at the vaulted ceilings, at the artwork from prominent Indigenous artists, at the recently repaired sections of the walls and floor, the paints and stains not an exact match, not as aged as sections around them. Those repaired places increased in frequency as they made their way to the back of the house, then into a suite of rooms at one end, a bedroom, sitting room, and office, the latter nothing like the cabin but exactly like it. Laptops open, files scattered across an oversize desk, a notepad with the chicken scratch Paris recognized.

"You can hang out here." Rena pointed at another door on the other side of the office. "There's a guest bedroom over there." He didn't mention that he and Mac had been sharing a bed for days. Rena's ringing phone saved him from the lie. "I need to take this."

"Sure thing," Paris said. While she took her call in the hallway, he circled behind the desk, figuring he could distract himself from what might be happening with Jason and Kai, with the only family he had left, by continuing his and Mac's work. Grabbing the stack of files he recognized as the detective's cold cases, he sank into the chair and pulled them closer, flipping through to see if any jogged a memory or rattled loose another soul. Nothing in the first few.

He shuttled the third case file to the no luck stack, then turned back to start on the fourth, only to be stopped cold by the black-and-white photo that had been wedged between the folders. Two men, their clothes from a time Paris had only read about in history books, the environs behind them unrecognizable, but he'd recognize the taller of the two men anywhere. Long, rangy body, dark hair and eyes, a sharp nose and that soft smile Paris couldn't get out of his head. Only in the photo it was directed at the man standing in his arms. Shorter, broader, laughing with his head thrown back, his light hair caught in the breeze. What had Mac said to make him do that? Who was he to Mac? When he'd finished laughing, had Mac drawn him back upright and kissed him? It was a simple picture, and yet one of the most romantic Paris had ever seen.

A gasp from the doorway crashed through Paris's spiraling thoughts, and for a panicked second, he thought it would be Mac standing there, but it was Rena, her eyes wide as she clutched her phone to her chest. "I've only seen that picture out of the safe once since Mac moved in here."

"It was between these file folders," he said, gesturing at the two stacks he'd made before staring again at the photo. "Who is he?"

"The reason Mac will push you away. Don't let him."

"What did Liam mean that Mac and I are bonded?"

"You need to talk to Mac about that."

He set the photo aside and splayed a hand over his chest. "It's why I can feel him here, isn't it?" Her eyes widened impossibly further, mouth rounding into an *O*. She must not have believed Liam when he'd said it, but she believed now. "I grabbed hold of him that night I almost died. I didn't know what else to do, but if he's already bonded to someone, if he didn't want to be bonded to me—"

"Have you felt him tug back?" Rena asked.

He held her gaze and nodded.

"Trust that," she said. "And trust yourself."

SEVENTEEN

PARIS WAS DREAMING about the ocean again. He was sitting on his favorite bench outside their condo building, watching the sun sink toward the horizon and the fog roll in. Below him, waves crashed against the cliffs, misting his face with sea spray and shaking the earth beneath his feet.

Shaking him.

"Come on, Paris. Wake up."

He opened his eyes to reality. No ocean, but an equally beautiful sight.

"There he is," Mac said as he kneeled beside him.

The morning sun streamed in through the window over his shoulder, and Paris squinted. "What time is it?"

"Early. Sorry about the sun," he said with a flick of his fingers at the glowing ball of light behind him. Brighter than Paris could ever remember seeing in his life. "This side of the house faces east."

Peeling himself off the folders and papers, scattering

some onto the floor, Paris propped an elbow on the desk to hold up his tired head and eked his eyes open wider, taking in the man before him. "You haven't slept." By now, Paris recognized the signs of a sleepless raven. "Long night?"

Hand on his knee, Mac lifted his dark gaze, and it swam with empathy, his aura pulsing indigo, brighter even than Liam's had that day at the cabin.

The rest of Paris's reality clicked into place, his heart drowning with it. "Is he—"

"Kai was right. Jason became a phoenix."

"How?"

"We don't know that yet. We'll ask him when he's conscious again. Kai's with him until then."

Reality shifted again, and Paris spun the chair to face Mac, sending more folders and papers to the floor. "Wait, Jason's alive? And Kai?"

"They're both alive," Mac said with a wide smile. "Was touch and go with Jason for a bit, but he should make—" Paris launched himself out of the chair and into Mac's arms. "Oof!"

Paris couldn't hold in the tears; with Mac, he thankfully didn't have to. He'd cried in his arms before, overcome with relief the morning he'd learned of his father's death. Relief racked his body again, but today, relief felt completely different. Before, his relief had been from fear, from his tormentor; a freedom Paris had never experienced, living under his abusive father's fist for twenty plus years. Today's relief was the opposite, steeped in love for the chosen family still with him and in gratitude for Mac and his team who'd rescued them. There weren't enough *thank yous* in the world, but Paris tried to give them all to Mac, a litany between broken breaths, as Mac leaned them against the desk and ran a hand up and down his spine, gentling him with soothing words.

But fast on the heels of relief came the overwhelming, shifting realities of the past two weeks. One of his best friends was a raven, the other was a phoenix, and he was just a human—in a world, a life, that was barely recognizable. In the arms of a different raven he wanted to get to know better. Where was his place anymore? With Kai and Jason, or with Mac and his team, or without any of them? How could he be anything but a burden to them all?

The questions, the doubts, stole his breath and left him gasping for air.

"Hey, hey, hey," Mac soothed as he held his face in his hands, his dark gaze inviting and calm, same as his words. "Breathe, Paris. Just breathe." A little gulp in. "They're fine." A slightly bigger gulp. "They're still your best friends." A full inhale. "And you can see them when it's safe." And finally, a deep one as Mac's thumbs swiped the tears from under his eyes.

"But Kai is safe with him?" he asked, voice wobbly.

"More than you can possibly know," he said, the same awe in his voice that had been there when Kai had arrived at the cabin. Tears pooled at the corners of his dark eyes, and when he hid them behind closed lids, a tear streaked down one cheek. He tilted forward, pressing their foreheads together. "That's how it's supposed to go."

Paris returned the earlier gesture, cupping his cheeks and offering comfort, whatever this man who'd saved him and his family needed. "What can I do? How can I help you?"

Mac's lower lip brushed against his. It was such a light touch, so soft and fleeting that Paris thought it incidental, but then Mac's lips pressed against his, firmer and longer, not an accidental brush. Paris was thrown into a tailspin, the desire that had been banked for days roaring to the surface. He hazarded a kiss back, and when Mac angled his face in Paris's hands so he could deepen it, Paris groaned and slid his hands into Mac's hair, clutching the dark strands when the tip of Mac's tongue teased his lips, asking for entrance. Paris didn't hesitate to open, to moan as Mac licked inside his mouth, tentative at first, but then growing in demand that fired every one of Paris's senses, that made him want to lie back and surrender all of himself.

Chasing that reality, he shifted in Mac's lap and tipped backward, taking Mac with him by the mouth, neither of them wanting to interrupt their greedy kisses. Mac threw out a hand to brace them on the way down—and planted on something that caused them to slip. He threw out the other hand, catching them before they hit the floor, laughter breaking their lips apart. Laughter Paris wanted to taste. But then Mac's gaze shifted to the side, catching on the thing that had caused them to slip.

The black-and-white photo of Mac and the other man.

Mac's laughter died, his skin paled, and he hastily untangled from Paris, scurrying to his feet so fast Paris nearly did hit the floor, only Mac's unerring manners saving him. "I'm sorry," he said as he helped Paris to his feet.

"Mac, wait."

"I need to get back to the team." He eyed the door like a man on fire. "We've got a lot to do before leaving for YB tonight."

He turned for the door, but Paris caught his wrist, halting his escape. "Thank you for bringing them back to me. They're the only real family I've ever had." *Before you* wanted to roll off his tongue, but he bit it back, letting the tug he made on their connection—their bond?—speak for him.

Mac's gaze snapped to his, then skittered away again. "They're valuable assets."

As Paris glanced again at the photo, he remembered Rena's advice—to trust what he felt and not let Mac push him away. No matter how their kiss had ended, it had been a breakthrough, especially for Mac who'd kept himself locked down—alone—for far too long. Taking Rena's advice, Paris pressed, a little. "That's not why you saved them, though, is it? You saved them for me." Paris lifted his hand and kissed the back of it. "Thank you."

"You're welcome," he replied, voice barely a whisper, but the tug Paris felt in his own chest as Mac left the room was louder than the thunderous waves back home.

———

Paris woke from his nap to the sense of someone watching him. He was on his side in the guest bed in Mac's quarters, the busy late night and tumultuous early morning having caught up with him by midday. He couldn't say when someone had joined him, but he was certain he wasn't alone. And given the pattern of that someone's breaths, the pine and earthy scent he'd come to associate with him, and the warmth spreading through his chest, Paris had a pretty good idea who it was beside him. No idea why, though, after the way he and Mac had left things that morning.

Instead of jumping in there, Paris led with something

easier, a joke to break the ice he hated around them. "Are you sure you're not a cat?" he said, not opening his eyes.

Mac chuckled. "Why would you think that?"

"You're like one of those domestic breeds. You know, the ones that wake their people up first thing in the morning by staring and pawing at them."

"Definitely not a cat. And it's definitely not morning."

Paris opened his eyes, meeting the dark ones across from him, then glanced past Mac and out the window, the waning sun casting the sky in hues of pink and purple.

"We're getting ready to head out," Mac said, drawing Paris's gaze back to him. "I didn't want to leave without saying goodbye. And without apologizing for earlier."

He hadn't had long to wallow after Mac had bolted that morning. Spying their uncle leave his office, Cherry and Abernathy had snuck in, apparently looking to raid the stash of candies Mac kept on top of his file cabinet. Finding Paris instead, they'd enlisted him in Operation Morning Sugar, first with the candies, then with the pancakes Liam was cooking in the kitchen. Paris had pitched in to help, the distraction welcome, as was Icarus when he'd appeared midmorning.

They hadn't needed to say anything, each of them swallowing the other in a hug. Holding tight. Theirs had initially been a transactional relationship, Icarus helping him feel not so lonely, Paris giving him what he'd needed to protect his sister, but friendship had grown between them. Icarus had been one of only a few people he'd been able to be himself around, and Paris had broken that trust, a betrayal—a mistake—that no matter what Mac said, he'd always feel guilty about. He'd tried to apologize, and Icarus had slapped a hand over his mouth and told him to "Shut it." Paris had been so shocked by the warmth and pulse he'd felt in his friend's hand that words had deserted him.

They'd deserted him again when a smiling Adam Devlin had joined them. He'd brought Kai with him, and if Paris had hugged Icarus hard, he hugged his best friend harder. He'd wanted to visit Jason too, but it wasn't safe for Paris to see him yet. He took their word for it but wanted a full accounting of the night's events, which Icarus had given in dramatic fashion, as was his way.

All of that activity and there'd been no Mac sightings. Had he eaten? Had he slept? When had he joined Paris in bed? And what did he have to be sorry for? "You don't have to apologize for anything," Paris said.

"I'm the one who initiated that kiss." His gaze strayed to Paris's lips a fleeting second before he flopped onto his back and stared at the ceiling. "I wanted it, even knowing it couldn't go anywhere."

He wanted it still if that ring of red bleeding into his usual aura of guilt and regret, empathy and grief was any indication. "Why can't it?" Paris asked, hoping for more of the story he'd only gotten glimpses of.

"I was in love once before."

"The man from the photo?"

"Hank," Mac said, his voice catching on the name. "He was my best friend." Pain streaked across his face, his brows furrowing and eyes slipping closed. "And I never told him."

Regret blew out every other emotion in his aura, and Paris reached across the inches between them, clasping Mac's hand. "I'm so sorry."

Mac swallowed hard and pressed on, like he needed to get the words out. "When my parents told us they were retiring, Hank told me I could do this. That I could be our clan's reaper."

"I'm sure he knew how strong you were, like I—"

"He was the first name on my list."

"Oh shit."

Paris regretted the curse as soon as it escaped his lips, but then Mac chuckled, the sound watery but amused, and some of the tension in his grip eased. "Yeah, oh shit." He turned on his side to face Paris again, their hands still joined. "I can't go into YB tonight not knowing if either of us will make it out alive."

"Do you think it'll be that bad?"

"In Yerba Buena, it already is. Up here, I don't know. So far just some skirmishes along the Bay's north edge, but there are no guarantees the violence from YB won't spill over. It already did earlier this month with Icarus and Adam. They'll be with me in YB, but Liam and Rena and all of my family will stay here, Kai and Jason too, and some of Jenn's pack. We have to be prepared for anything."

"I'll be fine," Paris said, squeezing his hand.

And then Mac practically squeezed his heart, pulling their hands to his lips and kissing the back of Paris's, repeating his gesture from earlier. "I can't be the one who has to deliver you. I can't go through that again."

Did that mean he couldn't—wouldn't—ever go through love again either? Because it would be a shame for someone who loved others so completely, who risked and tortured his own soul and body to make sure others' were at peace, to keep himself from experiencing total love and devotion in return.

To never let Paris try to be that person because Paris was already sure Mac was that person for him. Paris wanted that shot, wanted to give Mac everything he deserved, including a second chance at love. But short of putting that declaration out into the world, which would not do Mac any good on a day he clearly already dreaded, Paris settled for putting another out there, the only one that truly mattered. "We're all getting through this day—alive."

EIGHTEEN

PARIS HAD JUST FINISHED SHADING in some of the vine leaves he'd painted, adding yellow, brown, and red among the green, the valley of vineyards below awash with hues the likes of which he'd never seen in YB, when a voice came from behind him.

"How long have you been painting?"

He turned from the easel he'd set up under the pergola behind Mac's villa, as Adam called it, and found a new person approaching, someone he hadn't met since arriving at Monte Corvo. Not unusual—Liam was right, Mac's place really was a base of operations—but this was a person he'd remember. Dressed in ripped jeans, a faded black tee, and combat boots, the woman was pixie petite, with tan skin, hazel eyes, and a septum ring through her nose. Her long green hair was styled in barrel curls that bounced as she made her way along the edge of the reflecting pool between the house and pergola, tossing peanuts to the crows as she approached.

"All my life," he answered, once she stepped under the wooden trellis with him. "Even when I wasn't supposed to."

"No one should tell you not to do this," she said with a jut of her chin at his painting. "It's beautiful."

"It's beautiful here."

Smiling, she stepped to the end of the pergola and turned her face up to the sun. "It is, isn't it?"

"Did you grow up here? Are you part of Mac's family?" She was on the shorter side for a Kelley and lacked the dark eyes and straight noses they all seemed to have, but she shared his tan skin, a certain aesthetic in the dark clothing she wore, and the familiar signs of outward exhaustion, though with each second she stood in the sun, she seemed to brighten.

She lowered her face and turned back to him, hand extended. "I'm Mary, Icarus's sister."

"Oh!" The dyed hair and edgy aesthetic suddenly made sense. "I've heard a lot—" He slipped his hand into hers and lost his words, his eyes going wide and mouth rounding into an *O*. The energy that flowed from her, from her pure green aura, was blinding in its intensity. "What are you?"

"What do you think I am?"

Nature was on the tip of his tongue—he was sure of it—and on the heels of that realization, so many others fell into place. Mac and team fighting against Chaos, seemingly at the heart of Nature's cause, the sheer power of the magic around them, the way no one on the team referred to Mary by name or to what she so obviously was. "You're *her*."

One corner of her mouth kicked up, her smirk reminiscent of her brother's, as were her words. "People have always underestimated you, haven't they? He said you were smart."

"Icarus is too kind," he replied, and Mary hummed as she strolled back to the edge of the pergola, taking in another shot of sunshine before she claimed one of the loungers. "In fairness," Paris added as he finished dotting in the road that snaked between the rows of vines, "I didn't always lead with my head."

"The world would be an awfully sad place if that's all anyone did."

Reminded of his other friend who typically led with his heart, Paris set aside his brush and sank into the chaise opposite her. "Do you know how Jason is doing?"

"Good," she told him. "He's taken well to the phoenix. Much better than others we've rescued. Having Kai bonded with him helps."

"When can I see him?"

"In the next day or so, I think. We have to be sure he has control of the fire."

"And Adam and Icarus, and the rest of the team? We didn't need the infirmary, so that's a good sign, right?" After the team had left yesterday, he'd helped Monte and Chaz ferry additional supplies down to the overflow barrel room beneath the villa according to Icarus's instructions. A nursing student before he was turned, and still acquainted with those skills after becoming human again, Icarus was the unofficial team medic, thankfully not overseeing an infirmary full of injured this morning.

"No major injuries, so yes, that's a good sign, but it's been a long month already," she said. "And we're only halfway through it." Exhaustion leaked into her voice again, but after a deep inhale, she seemed to shake it off, to settle back into her world. "There's still work to be done in YB. They'll come back as their jobs are done." She shifted her gaze and smirk back to him. "Ask about who you want, Paris."

He splayed a hand over his chest, over where he'd periodically tugged the past twenty-four hours and always received one in return. And done the same when he'd felt Mac tug from his end. The connection still vibrated there, warm and alive. "I know he's fine."

"Doesn't make you not worried." Her smirk smoothed into a gentle smile. "He's fine, but it may take him longer. He's working with the other reapers in the city."

"Was it bad there?"

"Not as bad as it could have been if your father had still been alive. Or if you hadn't given us that list of potential allies. It put us ahead, on a lot of fronts."

"I'm glad it was helpful."

"I have some other questions." She stood and withdrew her phone, gesturing with it. "If you don't mind taking a look?"

"Of course not." He patted the spot on the chaise next to him, and she sat close so he could see the screen.

"You told Mac your father had maps. Do you remember these locations or any discussion of them?" She spread her fingers on the screen, zooming in, then moving the map to show him each spot in YB that had been marked with a red X.

"That one," he said, when she got to the marked spot at the southern edge of YB, a fog-shrouded stick of land that jutted into the Bay. He'd been there once with his father and even just standing by the car while his father met with a suited man near the shore, he couldn't remember a time in his life when he'd been so cold. Wind-whipped and fog-dampened, he'd crawled back into the car before his dad had returned. "He called it a 'transfer point.' I assumed he moved illegal goods through there. But I also didn't realize 'fuel stations' meant phoenixes."

"You had no reason to."

"So what is this transfer point?"

"Possibly an altar."

"For souls," he surmised, and she nodded. "The veil is thin there?"

"There," she said, "and these other spots." She swiped a finger across the screen and a different map appeared, this one showing areas outside of YB too. He recognized the spot on the ridge where Abigail's pack had been decimated, the spot in YB's Canyon Lands where he'd been nearly sacrificed, but there was another marked spot on the north edge of the Bay. "This is technically in Talahalusi, isn't it?" he asked.

"Yes, that's the Huimen Enclave. The areas along the water are tribal lands, mostly undeveloped coastal woods, but the outer portions have been settled and commercial-ized. Do you remember something there?"

"I heard my father on the phone once talking about potential investments there. But I don't know exactly where or what for, I'm sorry."

"It's still a lead, Paris." She patted his knee. "Good job."

"Is there a thin spot in the east? The shellmound, maybe?" Two in YB, one at the edge of Talahalusi on the Bay, and one on the ridge near Portola. It stood to reason there would be more spots around the Bay.

She smiled wider. "Two, actually, relatively close together, similar to the Stick and the area where we found you. One is near the Huchiun Enclave in the middle of the Bay and the other near the shellmound in Encinal. We control those, not Chaos."

"And in the south?"

Pain flickered across her delicate features, pinching the corners of her eyes and mouth, drawing attention to the wrinkles there Paris hadn't noticed before. She was older than she looked; magic at work. "La Purisima," she said, the pain likewise reflected in her voice.

"All the way down there?" There went the circle picture in his head and any connection to his dad. "My father wouldn't dare go there." The religious cultist would burn them all at the stake for believing in the supernatural, even as they worshipped their own sort. And they were too pious to consort with the likes of Vincent Cirillo.

But even if his circle theory was a bust, another picture formed in his head. "There's still a pattern," he told her, and gestured for the device. She handed it to him, and with a few taps on the device, he drew a sort of zigzag line on the map, connecting the dots. A hunting range. "Maybe we can use it to predict where the giants will strike next?"

"Good work, Paris," she said with a smile. "He was right." She took the device back and stood. "I'm going to run these locations and any in the path against your father's assets. See if we find anything close by."

Paris rose beside her. "You think he might have been funding the giants?"

"We know he was. We connected transfers from one of Vincent's bank accounts to the ridge giant we identified."

He raked a hand through his hair and sighed. "So it's not over today, is it?"

She shook her head, the barrel curls bouncing. "We think they're working toward a Samhain sacrifice. An attempt to open the veil so Chaos can come through." Another couple clicks on her device, and she turned the screen back to him. Multiple dots were clustered around several of the locations they'd already identified. "Missing persons reports, in and around the areas where the thin spots are."

"How does no one notice?"

"Because the culprit is the cart guy at the grocery store, or a doctor killing his patients, or"—another couple taps, and a photo of the giant he'd painted appeared—"the mechanic who worked on a pack member's bike."

"How do we beat this?" It all seemed so heavy and endless, one evil after another.

She looped an arm around his waist and gave him a sideways hug, quieting some of his unrest. "We work together as a team."

"And you're part of that team now," came Kai's voice from the edge of the pergola.

"I'll leave you to it," Mary said, drawing back and smiling up at Paris, sending him another wave of green comfort. "It was lovely to meet you, Paris."

She clomped off, headed back to the villa, tossing peanuts in her wake, and Paris gladly accepted the hug Kai offered in her place. "How's Jason?" Paris asked.

"Recovering. He'll be fine, thanks to you." He drew back, and they lowered onto one of the chaises beside each other. "How are you? With all this?"

"It's a lot. I mean that was just"—he gestured the direction Mary had disappeared into the house—"*her*."

"She's something else," Kai said with a chuckle. "Don't piss her off. She's more fiery than Icarus."

"I know they're not blood related, but the vibe is definitely siblings."

"Oh yeah, one hundred percent. Some folks are just on the same wavelength, you know? Connected, like they're destined to be in each other's lives."

Sounded familiar, especially about Paris's two best friends. He squeezed his friend's hand. "I'm so happy you and Jason are official now." Kai's cheeks heated, a shy smile turning up the corners of his lips. In all the ups and downs of the past two weeks, their happily ever after was a highlight. "I was getting tired of living in a constant state of would-you-two-just-kiss."

Kai laughed out loud, until he turned a mischievous, Jason-like smile on him. "Is that what you and Mac were doing before I showed up at the cabin?"

Paris's own cheeks heated. "We were just dancing." Close in each other's arms, the warmth of Mac's skin against his own, Mac's hand cupped around the side of his neck, the kiss that had almost happened then.

"But you want to be kissing?"

The kiss that had happened yesterday morning, that had lived rent-free in his head the past day and a half, replayed again, and Paris covered his face with his hands, groaning in frustration. "More than anything," he admitted, through his fingers. "But it's complicated. He's a reaper, and I'm just a human."

Kai rubbed a hand over his back. "You're not *just* anything, Paris."

He dropped his hands and spread one over his chest, over where his own heart beat for someone, truly, for the first time. But it wasn't the first time for Mac. "He's got a hole here, Kai, and I don't know if I or anyone can ever fill it."

"Maybe you're not supposed to. Maybe you're supposed to make your own place there."

NINETEEN

IT WAS a good thing Mac's kitchen was huge because everyone was in it this evening. Some of the team had returned last night, more had trickled in throughout the day, and the remainder were expected back any time now, including Mac and Liam. Rena and the kids were up from the mansion, Jason and Kai were up from the lake where Jason had been recovering, and Mary and Icarus had emerged from the barrel room where a handful of returning pack members had needed medical attention. All in all, a full house, with Cherry and Abernathy—and Jason, especially—making the meal Paris was attempting to prepare a challenge. Mostly the good kind, until Jason conjured up a ball of fire to "put a little char" on the homemade garlic bread Paris had just pulled from the oven, at which point the chef put his foot down.

Paris swatted his friend's big biceps and hip checked him toward the end of the massive island. "I love you, buddy, but you have got to get out from behind here, or Mac's not gonna have a mansion to come home to."

"Aww, come on, Paris," he whined. "Let me flamethrower it." He draped his massive body over the back of Paris's, his long arms dangling over his shoulders, glowing hands palms up in front of them.

"What's a flamethrower?" Cherry asked from where she sat on the other side of the island beside Kai.

Paris could feel Jason's grin against his cheek. "Me!"

"Jason!" he, Kai, and Rena all chided . . . to absolutely no avail.

If Mac reminded him of a domestic cat sometimes, then Jason was the epitome of a puppy, one of those big blond breeds that liked to throw itself into walls while endlessly chasing a ball. Good natured, carefree fun until said wall gave way. Or until Jason lit the pot holders on Paris's hands on fire, and Paris had to fling them to the floor and stomp the flames out.

"Oops," Jason said, grinning as he unwound from around Paris and stole the charred heel of the bread.

Paris hung his head back on a heavy sigh, dramatics turned up to Icarus levels, and everyone laughed, as he'd intended; the antics were good for lifting spirits, including his own. Food would do the same. He wisely waited until Jason was safely across the room before pulling the bubbling vegetable and cheese lasagna out of the oven. He'd just gotten the pans on the trivets and recovered in foil, holding ready until the rest of the team arrived, when Mary called from the hallway opening. "Hey, Paris, can I borrow you for a second?"

"Sure." He untied his apron, tossed it on the island, and wagged a finger at Jason as he crossed the room. "No more touching."

"No promises," he said with a wink from between a giggling Cherry and Abernathy.

"That's the trio of trouble right there," he said to Kai and Rena.

"We'll keep them in line," Rena assured him as she slid off her stool and took up kitchen guard duty. "That lasagna looks too good to end up on the floor."

Paris had to agree, the sweet potatoes, beets, and butternut squash creating layers that reminded him of the sunset he'd painted the other day. He hoped it tasted as good as it looked, once they got a chance to dig in. For now, he followed Mary into the parlor at the front of the house where Icarus, in combat boots, patchwork jeans, and a strappy tank, waited at the poker table by the corner window, his blue gaze fixed on the driveway out front. She slid into the chair behind the open laptop, beside her brother, and Paris claimed the one across from them. "Did you find something?" he asked.

"Prepare yourself," she said, then turned the laptop to face him. The warning should have been enough—he knew to expect the worst at this point—but the worst still took his breath away. Like at the ridge, the altar in the silent video had been reduced to rubble, though not as charred as the other crime scene. Fresher when the video had been taken. Blood still soaked the ground, witness corpses smoldered, and a pile of bones smoked atop the broken altar. Bones that could have been Paris at a different altar if not for Adam, Mac, and the rest of the team that had rescued him. He glanced away and swallowed hard, forcing the words out. "That's definitely a giant's altar," he said. "The Stick?"

"Yes," Mary replied. "Likely from the seventeenth. A source sent me this video."

He shifted his gaze to Icarus, whose brows had furrowed. "Not your team on the scene?"

"No," Mary answered for him. "I didn't want to add this to their plate. Or this . . ." She rotated the laptop back around, then after a few keystrokes, turned it back to Paris. "This is arial footage of the Huimen Enclave."

"One of the thin spots we talked about the other day."

She nodded, then, reaching around the side of the screen, clicked the right arrow key, and three dots appeared near the road that ran along the western edge of the enclave. "These are cold storage properties your father recently purchased in the area." Another click, and the map changed, showing a series of pathways that snaked through the peninsular territory. "These," Mary said, "are river-forged tunnels that run beneath the surface. The rivers are long gone, but the tidewater still comes and goes in the ones close to the water. The tunnels remain."

The horrible picture came together in Paris's head, and he covered his gaping mouth with a hand. "To chase the victims through."

"That's what we think." She met his gaze and cringed, apology in her hazel eyes. "There's more."

"Do I want to hear it?"

"Not really," Icarus answered, never taking his eyes off the driveway out the window.

"Tell me anyway."

"I cross-checked the localized missing persons cases for any known associations with your father." Mary clicked the forward arrow once more and three pictures appeared, name and descriptions in the captions underneath. "All paranormals. One who was also on Mac's list."

Paris didn't recognize any of them by appearance or by

name, but he recognized his father's MO. Three powerful paranormals—a shifter, a warlock, and a vamp—and one power-hungry human. "Dad used them up, then turned them over."

"Or he lured them to the giant," Icarus said.

"Or they betrayed him, and Dad turned them over." He snagged one of the poker chips from its center holder and flipped it through his fingers the way Atlas had taught him. Like his painting, the repetitive motion provided an outlet for his fear and anxiety so his mind could work. "This must be him. The same giant who took me."

"Maybe," Mary said. "Or maybe it's the ridge giant, who we know Vincent transferred funds to. It's likely your father had connections to multiple of them."

Paris tossed the chip aside and propped his elbows on the table, head in his hands. "Ugh. Could he be any more of an asshole?"

Icarus chuckled. "Go easy on him, babe." He pushed back from the table and circled it to Paris's side, giving his shoulder a squeeze. "Not sure he's used to the data dumps."

"I can handle it," Paris said, as he and Mary likewise rose. "I've been with Mac for two weeks."

Icarus's ginger brows raced north. "Have you now?"

"I didn't mean it like—"

His protest was interrupted by the roar of engines and gravel crunching under tires, but before he could lean to the side and peek out the window, Icarus grasped his chin. "Don't do anything heroic," he said, gaze fiery. "It usually ends in death."

"The way I hear it, you ran off and did something heroic, and you lived. Were reborn, in fact."

Icarus rolled his eyes. "What are we going to do with you?" He leaned forward and planted a smacking kiss on his cheek, and when he stepped back, Adam and Mac were waiting at the parlor door, while Liam, Jenn, and Abigail continued on to the kitchen, screaming children greeting their arrival.

Icarus greeted Adam by running across the room and jumping into his arms, the older man somehow not stumbling under Icarus's jacked body. "Fuck or food, baby?"

In answer, Adam turned on his heel and carried his lover toward the stairs, disappearing up them much to Mary's amusement, her laughter carrying her all the way to the kitchen, leaving only Mac and Paris in the parlor. Paris didn't run and jump at Mac; he didn't have to, Mac meeting him midstride, colliding in the middle of the room and wrapping their arms around each other, the bond between them solid. And singing.

"Welcome home," Paris said as he held Mac close, the raven seeming to want to burrow into him, hiding his face in the crook of his neck.

"I'm sorry," he mumbled against his skin, the words more felt than heard. "I didn't know it was going to take so long."

Paris cupped his cheek and tilted his face, catching his fading violet gaze. "Please quit apologizing for doing the thing that makes you you. You don't have to, not with me." A long exhale later, Mac let go of the remaining tension in his body and went practically limp in Paris's arms. In his care, right where Paris wanted him to stay. "You're here now, and that's all that matters. I've got you."

TWENTY

PARIS WOKE to sun on his face and heat at his back, to soft skin and softer kisses along his shoulder blades, to pine and earth and Mac's breath on his nape. A dream, then, one he wanted to stay in for a change. An alternate reality in which, after Paris had finished cleaning up after dinner and returned to his room, he'd found Mac asleep in the guest bed he'd used since arriving at Monte Corvo. He'd crawled in with him, and sometime during the night, the man he was falling for had wrapped around him, was touching him, kissing him, hard for him.

Paris rutted back against Mac's erection, and the dream Mac grunted. Then glided a hand down Paris's side, from his shoulder, along the curve of his flank, over his hip, and held him there as he rocked closer, dick notching along Paris's crack, leaking through the damnable fabric between them. And fucking hell if Paris didn't want their boxers gone so Mac could shove inside him to the hilt. Fill him full. He leaned his head back on Mac's shoulder, groaning. "Fuck, I need you."

Mac's hand on his hip shifted forward, and for a fleeting second Paris thought it was on the way to where he wanted it most, to give his aching cock the relief he craved, but then Mac coasted it up his torso instead. Up, up, up, until he clasped his chin and angled his face to look over his shoulder. "Open your eyes, Paris."

He obeyed—and jolted. Not a dream. So not a dream. Mac's hair was a mess, a thin ring of violet circled his blown wide pupils, and the color was high on his cheeks, a dark pink like the spider web of desire splintering his aura, cracking through the usual black and blue.

"You brought me home," Mac said, and Paris felt the pull in his chest. "Every time I crossed the plane, I had a reason to come back. I've never had that before. Some part of me always felt adrift, the worst on the day of the Rift and each anniversary since. Like I might just drift away too, into the cold, but that didn't happen this time. I came back, because of you."

"Because we're bonded," Paris said, as he sent a pulse of understanding—of acceptance—along the connection between them.

Gasping, Mac released his chin and splayed his hand over Paris's chest, right where Paris felt their connection. "You grabbed hold, and now I can't let go either." Forehead to his temple, he nuzzled the side of Paris's face, lips brushing the corner of his mouth. "I'm terrified, Paris, but I can't fight this. I don't want to."

"I don't want you to fight it." He turned over in Mac's arms so he could hold his face, so Mac could see—would believe—the conviction in his gaze as he repeated his promise from last night. "It's my turn now. I've got you."

Mac groaned, relief made audible, that same emotion Paris was getting used to thanks to him, and then his lips were on Paris's, hard and greedy, forcing Paris's apart so he could spear his tongue inside his mouth. Paris sucked him in deeper, threw a leg over his hip, and hauled his body closer, their cocks bumping. The needy whine that rumbled up from Mac's chest was a sound Paris wanted to wallow in, wanted to hear over and over again. Better to be had with Mac on top, grinding down on him. Using his leg over Mac's hip, he moved to roll him, but Mac caught himself before falling through Paris's open legs, his features pinched. "Paris, I—"

"What is it?"

"I don't know how to do this."

"Stop overthinking." It was a habit of Mac's, consideration from all angles. Good for a detective, less so for a lover. Paris wanted him to let go and just feel this, feel them.

"No." He shook his head and bit his bottom lip as red climbed his cheeks again. "I don't know how to do *this*," he said with a pointed glance down to where their cocks were straining between them.

Oh, fuck . . . "Are you saying you're a virgin?"

He hid his flaming face in the crook of Paris's neck. "I've only been attracted to one other person, and I didn't tell him. We didn't get this far."

"Hank?"

He nodded, and by the hitch of his torso, by the grief and regret that flared in his aura, the mention had brought his former loss to the surface again.

Paris carded his fingers through his hair and kissed his temple. "One, you have nothing to be embarrassed about, and two, I'm sorry, for both your sakes. I could see in that picture how much you loved each other. You should have gotten this chance with him."

Mac lifted his face from his neck, eyes glassy, and for a split second, Paris thought he was going to pull away, that he might leave the bed altogether, but then he shifted and sank between his thighs, fully on top of Paris, his elbows braced on either side of his head, fingertips soft at his temples, like that first time Paris had woken to his gaze. "I don't know how to do any of this. I swore I never would again. But I want to, with you. Just please . . ." He lowered his forehead against Paris's, their noses bumping, lips brushing. "Please be patient with me."

"I've got you," Paris vowed a final time before acting on his words, closing the distance between their lips and sending a wave of comfort and care down the bond between them.

Pink and red cracked through Mac's aura again, brightening as Mac deepened their kiss, as he began to explore, a hand roving down Paris's side and under his thigh, hitching it higher and bringing their cocks back into contact. And when Paris rocked up this time, Mac countered, rutting with a hungry growl that lifted goose bumps along Paris's skin and made his dick ache.

"Fuck, yes," Paris groaned.

"Show me what you like."

He encouraged Mac to keep rutting, to keep questing, a hand in Mac's hair guiding his lips down his throat and to all the places he loved being teased. Behind his ear, the divot at the base of his throat, along his collar bones and around his nipples. He was writhing beneath him in no time, his dick a sticky mess in his boxers. Desperate to get them the rest of the way undressed, he skated a hand down Mac's back and inside the waistband of his boxers. "Let's get these off."

Mac helped shove his own off, then Paris's, and when they came back together, bare, Mac trembled. Then damn near jolted off the bed when Paris wrapped a hand around both their cocks. "Oh, fuck."

"Not there yet." Paris smirked as he stroked them together, smearing precome between them. He wasn't usually such a bossy bottom, but he was the more experienced one here, and the less Mac thought, the more he just felt, the better this would be for both of them. "Soon," he promised. "And just to be clear, once you get inside me, I fully expect you to blow in two seconds flat. And that's a compliment to me; it says nothing about you."

"But what about *you*?" Mac gritted out as he tunneled into Paris's fist, dragging his cock along Paris's. "I have no idea what I'm doing, but it feels good. And I want it to feel good for you too."

"Oh, it will." He captured Mac's lips again, dragging him into a plundering kiss, only coming for air when the pace of Mac's thrusts came too fast, too close. "I'm going to make you come, and then after, you're going to suck me off while you play with the come you leave in my ass."

Mac's eyes grew wide. "Fuck, you're amazing."

Pride swelled, Mac always so good at doing that for him, at making him feel like he was more than the fool he'd always been led to believe was his fate. In this man's life, in his arms, he could be so much more. "I'm about to show you how amazing." Grinning, he planted an elbow in the bed beneath him and flipped them so Mac was on his back, Paris straddling his hips.

And fuck, as much as Paris wanted to sink onto his dick, all that rosy tan skin on display had him leaning forward and kissing a similar path to the one he'd led Mac on earlier. From the sensitive spot behind his ear, down either side of his neck to the dip where his sharp collar bones met, then across every inch of his chest, giving each nipple extra attention, Mac seeming to especially enjoy it when Paris alternated between nipping the sensitive nub and running the flat of his tongue around it. He shivered and moaned under Paris's touch, begging for more among a litany of curses.

He'd begun a trek south, covering more of Mac's torso with kisses, when the raven grasped his shoulders and hauled him up, panting "About to come" against his lips. "Need to be inside, please."

"Grit your teeth," Paris said, before spitting in his hand, then reaching behind himself to stroke Mac's length, smearing it with the precome there before shoving his own slick fingers into his hole, hastily working himself open. They'd do more prep next time, he'd let Mac have all day exploring his hole if he wanted, but if the tightness in Mac's jaw was any indication, two seconds was being generous.

"Okay, breathe with me," he coached, waiting for Mac to match his inhale, his exhale before he took Mac in hand and slid down onto him, inch by glorious inch, until he was buried to the hilt.

Mac's hands clutched his thighs. "Fucking hell, Paris," he cursed as he closed his eyes and arched his neck, head jammed into the pillow.

Paris took advantage of the opportunity, leaning

forward and licking a stripe up the column of his throat. "No, baby, this is you fucking me, and it's far from hell."

"So far," Mac keened as Paris lifted up, then slammed back down on his dick.

Three more times, an admirable couple of seconds longer than Paris had estimated, before all of Mac arched, his back bowing off the bed as his warmth flooded inside Paris.

As the bond between them flooded with so much more.

Desire. Gratitude. Hope. Love.

The last one making Paris gasp, making him wobble off balance.

And in the next blink, he was on his back, the shifter previously beneath him flexing his speed, hovering over him with burning violet eyes. "Let me know if I do something wrong." And then he was kissing a path down Paris's torso, making a beeline for his dick. He didn't take long getting there, didn't approach with the same caution he had their first kiss. No, he swiped his tongue around the head once, then swallowed him until he gagged. A quick readjustment later, and he was sucking his cock like he was made for it. And then his fingers entered the picture, pushing into his dripping hole, and Paris was lost.

To the hot mouth greedily taking his cock, to the demanding fingers that found the sensitive spot inside him and worked it relentlessly, drawing pleas of "harder" and "faster" out of him, to the bond that sang between them, knitting their souls together tighter, spinning the threads of pink and red throughout Mac's aura.

And as Paris's orgasm barreled into him, as he squeezed shut his eyes and gave himself over to the explosion of pleasure, he was sure if he looked into a mirror, if he could see his own aura, it would be the color of the sunsets he loved to paint so much. Red and pink, his feelings for Mac, orange for the power and momentum he'd put in Paris's hands, and yellow for the confidence and hope he would have never found without him.

TWENTY-ONE

PARIS WAS COLD.

Not as cold as he had been locked in that awful freezer, but down here in the violet dark, it wasn't much better.

Violet.

He froze and reevaluated his surroundings. Not pitch-black, a purple hue coloring the edges. A dream—or memory—he had fallen into. Whose was it? And where was it?

He inhaled and smelled earth and brine, shifted his feet and felt water lap at his ankles, and when he stretched his arms out wide, his fingertips brushed walls of dirt and mud, tree roots and rock.

The tunnels beneath the Huimen Enclave. While he'd never been there before, he was sure that was where he was now, in the network of underground tunnels Mary had shown him.

Splashing echoed from somewhere in the tunnels, growing louder, coming closer. Paris flattened himself against one side of the tunnel and inched along the wall, careful not to splash, until he found the next junction and rounded the corner, plastering himself to a different cold dirt wall.

And waiting.

The splashing grew louder, accompanied by that horrible voice Paris would never forget. "You can't save her, warlock!" bellowed the giant who'd tortured and tried to sacrifice him. Who couldn't see him now, Paris reminded himself as the splashing footsteps stopped right outside the tunnel where he hid. He was here for a reason; he had to keep his eyes and ears open for clues.

He peered around the corner and spied two people in the main tunnel, the warlock's green magic faint but bright enough to light his and the woman's face. He recognized Quinn Paxton from the photo Mary had shown him—tan skin, dark hair, green eyes, compact body—but he was all skin and bones, his hair limp, his eyes dull, and his clothes too big for his emaciated frame.

Paris didn't recognize the woman with him. She wasn't much older than him, with tan skin and big brown eyes, and like the victim from the Portola parking lot, her face was bloodied and bruised. But unlike that woman, this stranger was pregnant, one arm in a makeshift sling, the other wrapped protectively over her round belly.

"Go," Quinn said, with a nod toward the tunnel where Paris hid. "I'll hold him off."

"How?" she said. "You're weak already. Vincent made sure of that."

"I'm strong enough to give you a head start."

"You're mine," the giant shouted, ever closer. "Both of you."

"Please, Pati, go," Quinn urged the woman.

Pati, Pati, Pati, Paris repeated to himself, committing her name to memory.

She clasped Quinn's hand in hers. "I'll name him Pax, after you."

He laid his other hand on her belly, a mist of green shimmering around them. "It would be my honor. Now go!" With a final sideways hug, he directed her into the tunnel, and she splashed past Paris, into the dark.

Just in time as the giant sent a barrage of fireballs down the tunnel. They exploded against a shield of green, one after another until the giant was right in front of Quinn. The worst night of Paris's life, his nightmares since, come to life again.

"Paris."

He whipped his gaze to the warlock who was staring straight at him, his mouth moving, forming urgent words. "Help her," he pleaded, a second before a fireball sizzled through the shield of magic and swallowed him whole.

———

Paris would have lurched to sitting in bed if not for the man draped over him, Mac's thigh thrown over his and an arm slung across his middle. Mac's breaths blew steadily over his chest, his familiar snores the first thing that penetrated the blood whooshing in Paris's ears as he returned to this reality, only a few hours since he and Mac had fallen back asleep after making love. His mind—and body—wanted to go back there, to that perfect place of warmth and connection, but he didn't have time. He needed to get the details down before they flitted away.

He scooted out from under Mac, a testament to the

raven's exhaustion that he didn't wake, then slipped the rest of the way out of bed, pulling on his sweats and sneaking out of the room, closing the door behind him. He hustled through Mac's office to the sitting room where he kept his painting supplies and gathered what he needed, setting up an easel in the corner and getting to work, painting the faces and places of his nightmare.

Once every detail had made it to canvas, Paris laid down his brush and returned to the bedroom. He'd been planning while painting, a means to rescue Pati coming together in his head. But he stalled over the threshold, watching Mac's beautiful body rise and fall, his tan skin warm and rosy in the late morning sun. The aura around him flowing blue and violet, red bleeding through from the rim, and at the very center, a new green orb. The man who'd helped everyone else first the past two weeks, who'd done everything Nature had asked of him, was finally taking a much-needed rest.

How could Paris wake him? How could he burden him with more? How could he ever convince Mac to let him do what he had to? Paris could take it from here, thanks in no small part to the confidence Mac had instilled in him. *I've got this*, he'd told Mac. Now he had to prove it—to Mac, to himself, to everyone who'd ever thought him a fool.

PART TWO

MAC

TWENTY-TWO

MAC WAS HOT, a long-lost sensation, so much of his reaper's existence spent in the cold ether between planes. He wrestled with the tangled sheets, kicking them down so he could roll onto his back, the other side of the bed blissfully cool.

He bolted upright.

Paris wasn't here. Hadn't been for some time, judging by the coolness of the sheets under his hand.

Paris, who had grabbed hold of his soul that night on the altar and hadn't let go.

Paris, who had spent the past two weeks surprising him, impressing him, understanding him.

Paris, who had held him, cared for him, offered him something he'd thought lost forever.

Mac closed his eyes, felt for the bond between their souls, and tugged.

And got no tug in return.

He shot out of the bed.

Suppressing the panic that threatened, he surveyed the

room through a detective's eyes. Paris's sweats were gone, his bag of clothes too, and outside the window, the sun shone bright. Two in the afternoon, according to the bedside clock.

Spinning on his heel, he ran into the office. Nothing out of place.

He ran farther, into the sitting room, and skidded to a halt. Two easels stood by the window, and on them, canvases in violet.

On one, an earthen tunnel, a face from his list, a crumbling shield of green magic between the warlock and the giant who'd almost murdered Paris.

On the other, a pregnant woman Mac had never seen before, and in the corner of the canvas, where Paris usually signed his paintings, two words: Help her.

———

A full house last night and nary a one of them to be found today. Monte and Chaz were in the infirmary monitoring the several injured they'd brought to the mountain yesterday, but otherwise, Mac found no one on the main floor or in the upstairs rooms.

And no sign of Paris.

He stood in the parlor where Paris had held him last night and wondered if this was all a bad dream. But even in those the past two weeks, in every trip he took across the veil, Paris was with him, in that place he'd carved for himself at the center of Mac's world. Where Mac had sworn he'd never let anyone in again.

Especially someone on his list, which Paris had been since the night they'd rescued him. Mac hadn't told anyone, hadn't wanted to explain why he didn't take Paris's soul through the veil. He'd known Paris didn't deserve the same fate as his father, but at the time, he hadn't known why. Hadn't known how to explain his certainty to anyone else. So instead, he'd secreted Paris away in Encinal, then Calera, as far from death as possible and as far from him and the fate Mac had barely survived before. But he hadn't been able to stay away, drawn by the man and the bond between them, and now the same fate was chasing him again, closer each day he fell a little more in love with Paris Cirillo.

"Fuck!" How had he let this happen? Any of it, all of it. He knew better. He'd pushed everyone away for decades, keeping only a handful of trusted friends, a stack of cases no one else wanted, and the memory of a love that had never had a chance to bloom. But then the fool son of a mobster had grabbed hold of his soul, had proved he was anything but a fool, and now . . . "Fuck!" he cursed again as he plowed his hands through his hair.

"We need to find the woman in the tunnels."

Mac spun the direction of Mary's voice, finding the green-haired pixie in the doorway. "Where's Paris?"

"Where he needs to be."

Fuck her riddles.

He tore off past her and out the front door, took to wing, and scoured the grounds for any sign of Paris or the team he needed to help find him.

A flash of pale skin and red hair caught Mac's eye, and he sailed to the edge of the woods near Adam's favorite meadow. Needing his words, he shifted right into a dead sprint toward where he'd glimpsed Icarus, heedless of the noise he was making, footfalls heavy and words louder. "Adam!" he shouted. "Icarus!"

He crashed into the meadow, into what must have been an intimate moment, the two of them clutching clothes to their fronts, but then Adam took one look at him, handed his pistol to Icarus, and rushed to his side, hand on his arm. "Mac, what's wrong?"

The warmth of his hand—the kind of warmth Mac had felt when he woke, that he'd fallen asleep to in Paris's arms, that he might never feel again—brought reality crashing down, and Mac with it, falling to his knees and burying his face in his hands. "Paris is gone."

Adam kneeled beside him. "What do you mean Paris is gone?"

"Babe." Icarus *tsk*ed. "Give him a minute to breathe. And give me my skirt."

Mac snarled at the blue-eyed former vampire. "Your sister."

Icarus rolled his eyes as he and Adam dressed. "What about her?"

"She knows where he is, and she wants us to rescue someone else."

"Maybe Paris doesn't need rescuing."

"Mac," Adam said as he shoved his gun in the waistband of his jeans, then crouched in front of him again. "Start from the top."

"You're in love with him," Icarus said from behind his mate, and Mac's snarl escalated to a full-on growl.

"Babe," Adam said, returning the earlier *tsk*. "Not helping."

Icarus just shrugged, insolent as ever. "Wait until Robin hears this."

Robin—that was who they needed, on multiple fronts.

The time for revenge and wild goose chases was over. "Get him back here," Mac said to Adam. "We need a tracker."

Adam didn't argue. They'd been partners on the force for years; yes, emotions were running high, but tactically, they could read each other like a book. "Call Jenn," he said, handing Icarus his phone. "Tell her to call the pack. Robin won't ignore it. Not after last time." The last time Robin had ignored the pack call, his twin sister, Adam's late wife, had been killed along with their husband. As Icarus stepped a few feet away, phone to his ear, Adam turned back to him. "What happened?"

Mac rocked back on his ass and accepted the shirt Adam handed him, spreading it over his lap. "He must have had a dream. I woke up and he was gone, but there were paintings. One was of the giant who took him, faced off with a warlock from my list in some kind of underground tunnel. The other was—"

"Pati Miwra," Mary said, walking toward them under Icarus's arm. "She's the daughter of one of the Huimen tribe's leaders. She carries an eagle. She'll name them Pax, after her savior."

"An eagle?" Adam gasped. "I thought they were gone."

The reappearance of eagles was significant. Perhaps more so, though, was this one's name. "Pax, as in *peace*?" Mac asked.

Mary nodded, and Mac propped his elbows on his knees, head in his hands. She was right; they had to rescue this woman. But fuck, where was Paris, and why couldn't he feel his soul?

Mary laid a hand on his shoulder, and a wave of warmth washed through him, holding back the threatening chill. "Kai and Jason are with him. He's going to help us find Pati. You need to believe in him."

He hung back his head and stared at the woman with all the answers, the deity who held his fate, his heart, in her hands. "Why didn't he wake me?"

"Because you wouldn't have let him do what he needs to do."

"Which is what?"

"Be Vincent Cirillo's son."

TWENTY-THREE

ROBIN ROSE FROM HIS CROUCH, wiping his muddy fingers on his denim-clad thigh. "Tracks are fresh," he said, voice low. "She's still in here."

"And the giant?" Mac asked, likewise whispering.

"Him too." He lifted his headful of rusty-blond hair, sniffed the air, then veered into a narrow tunnel to the right, barely wide enough for the coyote shifter's shoulders. Only Icarus was a match for Robin's size, which made him a brick wall when he halted on a dime, Adam crashing into the back of him with a curse.

"Fuck, Robin, a little warning."

"Sorry," he said, not sounding sorry at all. "Forgot you were human again."

He'd come when called, exactly as Adam had predicted, and when he'd found out why, he'd bitched the entire afternoon and evening they'd had to wait for low tide and the cover of darkness. Never mind the lives and lasting peace on the line; he'd heard *Paris Cirillo* and had been ready to bolt right back out the door, back to chasing the warlock he blamed for his sister's death. From Mary's and Paris's comments about Atlas, from what Mac had witnessed with his own eyes the night they'd battled Vincent, Mac was beginning to think there was more to Atlas than they realized, but Robin was a dog with a bone and on one side of that bone was the warlock's name and on the other was Robin's own guilt. Good luck stopping him; they only had him for a blink and then he'd be gone again. They just had to deal with his surliness in the meantime because they needed their best hunter.

"What is it?" Mac said.

Robin extended a hand to the wall, then jerked it away like he'd been burned. He glanced over his shoulder, golden eyes skipping past Adam to him. "Your precious human's been here too."

"How?" Mac said, surprise amplifying his voice louder than intended. He lowered it again and asked quietly, "When?" According to Mary, Paris had gone to the Cirillo compound in YB. He hadn't actually been here in the tunnels beneath the Huimen Enclave.

"I don't know," Robin sniped. "This is your kind of magic. Not mine."

Mac put his hand to the wall, in the same spot Robin had, and felt the soul that had been hidden from his for the past six hours. He yanked on the soul bond—and Paris yanked back. Mac nearly fell to his knees, only the wall he leaned against holding him up. Paris had been here; Paris was still on this plane. Thank fuck.

And just as Mac recognized Paris's soul, he also recognized the viewpoint of the paintings he'd left behind. "This is where he watched from." And given how he'd painted Pati, looking back over her shoulder, she'd run right past him. "Pati went this way," he said, shoving off the wall and charging ahead, keeping his footfalls light, the mud further dampening the sound of their movements.

The next tunnel junction was a three-way, and above it, a chute in the ground that had metal rebar rungs leading up to a hatch door, the lights on the keypad beside it glowing purple. The way she'd programmed it. "Paris installed the hack," Mac said, pride tipping up the corners of his lips. He'd gotten into the compound and into Vincent's office, then into the safe he'd broken into countless times before to steal from his father's supply of Daylight. The same safe where Vincent stored his laptop that Mary now had control of.

"So," Adam said. "That's one cold storage facility cleared. Stands to reason, the door that leads to the second one, which should be farther down that tunnel"—he pointed to the far-right one—"should also be cleared." Jenn and Abigail were each leading surface teams, rescuing any victims still held in the facilities Vincent had owned on the eastern side of the border road.

"Meaning the third," Mac said, referring to the facility on the other side of the road, down the far-left tunnel, "is waiting and ready." For them to herd a giant into so they could capture him on the surface. Liam and Icarus were standing by to lead that charge, *after* their trio got Pati out of here alive.

"And the woman is down that one," Robin said, pointing straight ahead.

"The giant?" Adam said.

Robin shook his head. "I lose him here. Must have turned back."

"They hunt their victims," Mac said. "He'll be back."

"Let's go, then," Adam said, poorly disguising the shiver in the detective-turned-vigilante's voice.

Robin led them down the middle tunnel, Mac following behind Adam, somewhat less careful now, Mac also sensing another presence, smelling her and the unborn shifter as they snaked farther into the earth, coming to another junction.

And meeting a wall of fire.

Mac shifted on instinct and so did Robin, the crack of bones one second, a giant rust-blond body on all fours the next. Beneath him, Adam drew his pistol and leveled it at the knees of the large bald man they knew as the giant from the ridge, in human form no doubt to disguise his scent or to give the pregnant woman behind him the illusion of a chance. Not the giant they were expecting but no less dangerous, balls of fire hovering over his hands.

Backed into a dead end, hunted to within an inch of her life, Pati was still in jeopardy. A shot fired in the giant's direction could hit her too, and while the silver bullets in Adam's gun might not kill her, they would kill the eagle she carried. Mac needed to create more space between the giant and Pati if they had any hope of saving her and themselves.

Adam realized it too, gesturing up with his gun and rolling out from under Robin, staying between the coyote's big body and the tunnel wall, eyeing a path to get behind the giant with Pati, if Mac could carve out that extra space for him.

He flew high, wings spread wide, but rather than attack the giant's eyes and possibly push him backward, closer to Pati, he flew over and behind him, then dug his talons into his neck and wrapped his wings around his head, blinding him with feathers and pain, hoping like hell the fireballs he flung as he staggered forward missed his friends. And gave them the room they needed to maneuver—fast—because Mac felt the energy inside the giant sizzling. At any moment, he would transform into the nightmare of Paris's paintings, and none of them would survive.

Two shots fired and the giant lurched, sank, and Mac released him, flying back and up, out of Robin's way as the coyote slammed into the giant from behind and took him to the ground, pinned him there long enough for Adam to run past with Pati under his arm. The giant roared, the tunnel walls trembling, and while the plan had been to herd him out, at the rate the earth around them was crumbling, they just needed to get out alive.

Mac sounded the alarm, a shrill *KRAA* his team knew well. Robin banged the giant into the ground one more time, enough to momentarily daze him, then took off after Adam and Pati, Mac flying overhead. Watching as the coyote shifted midstride so that when they reached Adam and Pati beneath the exit chute, he could help Adam lift her high enough to reach the rungs and start to climb toward the hatch. Adam stayed right behind her, reaching a long arm around her to key in the code Mary had given them. They shoved open the hatch door and cold air rushed into the tunnel, just as hot air began to build beneath Mac's wings, orange light and thundering steps closing in.

Mac cried again, as much a "GO!" as he could manage in raven form. Robin got the message, quickly scaling the rungs next, Mac providing cover behind him as the giant, in full monstrous form, charged their direction, hands of fireballs out, ready to defend himself. Mac did the unexpected —swooping low, talons digging into the bullet wounds behind the giant's knees, driving the silver bullets deeper, speeding along what the rush of magic had temporarily slowed. The giant staggered into the fragmenting wall, his weight dislodging chunks of mud and limestone.

"Mac, let's go!" Adam called from overhead. "She's gonna blow it."

He dodged the giant's flailing arms and sailed up and out the chute, Robin slamming shut the hatch door just as the earth heaved, Nature answering the call like Mac had seen her do weeks ago at the Canyon Lands.

KRAA!

"Run!" Robin shoved a shoulder under Pati's armpit, Adam under her other, and they sprinted out of the cold storage unit, out of the building, and toward the road, Mac sailing above them with a flock of corvids, their group reaching stable ground not a moment too soon.

Nature gave a final, powerful jolt and the land on the other side of the road sank, the tunnel walls collapsing into a massive sinkhole and, with any luck, swallowing the giant for good.

TWENTY-FOUR

TWENTY-FOUR AGONIZING HOURS LATER, Mac sailed toward the Sunset Hill condo building that earlier that month had been impenetrable to their team. Only Icarus had been able to get through then, and only after baiting Atlas into letting him in. But thanks to Paris's list of potential allies in Vincent's ranks, thanks to his intelligence and courage, Mac was able to slice through the shimmer of blue magic that shielded the building, wielded by a warlock who had previously used that very magic against Mac and his team. Paris had been right; Vincent had had his knee to more necks than just his own son's.

As soon as he was inside the shield, he felt it—Paris's soul woven with his. Whatever magic was in the shield had temporarily masked it, but it was still there, stronger than ever. He circled the building inside the shield, surveying with his own eyes what communications from inside had told him. Paris was safe; he'd declared himself the heir and taken control of his father's empire.

For now.

He'd no doubt be contested, but not from the inside by the look of it. From the outside, yes, that was already happening, but it appeared he'd made more friends inside than he'd let on given how quickly Vincent's remaining operatives had fallen in line. The detective part of Mac had a long list of questions, but the raven, the soul that had improbably found a second mate, just wanted Paris back in his arms.

On his second lap around the building, he spied Kai waiting in a halo of light on the rooftop, a folded stack of clothes under one arm. Mac coasted to a landing at his feet, shifting in the space between one breath and the next. "Where's Paris?"

"Waiting for you," Kai said. He held out the clothes and a pair of athletic flops. "Did everyone get back okay last night?"

"All in one piece." Mac donned the charcoal pants and lavender dress shirt, leftovers from Atlas judging by the lingering warlock stench and the too-short inseam and sleeves, Atlas a good half foot shorter than him. Whatever, he only needed clothes long enough to reach Paris's condo a floor below. He slid his feet into the flops, then glanced back up at Kai. "Take me to him."

He opened the rooftop door and led them into the stairwell. "Did they find anyone else at the cold storage facilities?"

"One was empty," Mac told him as they descended. "The missing vampire and shifter were in the other."

"It's a good thing Paris is here, then."

"How do you mean?"

"Who knows how many more victims Vincent has squirreled away. Now we have an inside line."

Mac opened his mouth to argue—there were less dangerous ways to gather intel—but then Kai opened the door to the penthouse floor and all of Mac's arguments vanished, his gaze landing on the man waiting at the end of the hall.

Paris had traded his sweats for an impeccably tailored suit, the dark fabric tucked in all the right places, the black dress shirt open at the collar, accentuating the long column of his throat. The whole ensemble showed off the tall, toned figure that would be walking runways in a different era, in a different place, if Paris hadn't been born into YB's ongoing war between Nature and Chaos. And to a cruel man who'd overshadowed him, abused him, and held him down his entire life. With the weight of Vincent gone, Paris was a different man than earlier surveillance photos had let on, pictures in which he was always in a suit and tie, his smile tight, his hair slicked back, his brown eyes dull. *A pretty face*, Icarus had once said.

The Paris in front of Mac now was more than just a pretty face. He was vibrant, his smile wide, his dark hair in waves around his face, his brown eyes swirling with warmth and affection—desire—that pulsed along the bond between them. He was everything Mac wanted.

A different door opened, and Mac smelled shifter, felt heat, and was a blink away from shifting himself when Paris's "Mac, no!" collided with the "Jason, no!" from behind him.

"It's just me!" Jason let go of the door and lifted his hands, palms out. "Sorry, man, I heard voices."

Kai slid between them, shoving Jason back into the condo that would've been Atlas's, if Mac recalled Icarus's hand-drawn blueprints correctly. "For a smuggler, you have the absolute worst timing." He glanced over his shoulder at Mac, then Paris. "Let us know if you need anything." Then slipped into the condo, closing the door behind him and Jason.

Swinging his gaze back to Paris, Mac opened his mouth again, only to be cut off by Paris's raised hand. "I know you're mad, and I'll explain and apologize, but I'd rather we not argue and do all that in the hall where folks can hear us."

Mac nodded; he didn't want to stay in the hallway either, but not for the reasons Paris thought. As soon as they were inside Paris's condo, as soon as Paris turned the lock on the door, Mac spun and shoved him against it, claiming the mouth he'd gone too long without. Paris groaned, tipping back his head as he rocked his hips, and Mac's lips slipped lower, to his jaw, then his throat, tasting skin and sucking on the pulse point that hammered in his neck, a sign of the blood that still flowed through his veins, the life that for a time yesterday Mac had feared taken.

Life he needed to be connected to again. "We'll argue about it later," he panted, tearing Paris's gaping shirt wider and splaying his hands over his chest, over warm skin reddening more as a blush climbed toward his neck. Mac nuzzled into all that heat, kissing and licking to the melody of Paris's groans, to the insistent rock of his hips, his cock hard against Mac's thigh, Mac's own straining inside his pants. "Right now, I just need to be inside you. To be . . ."

Paris grasped his chin and lifted Mac's gaze to his burning brown one. "To be what, Mac?"

"Where I belong, with you."

He had his work, his friends, his family, but he'd only truly belonged once before. He didn't think he'd ever find that feeling again, had actively avoided it, afraid the loss that came after would well and truly destroy him a second time, and then this beautiful, surprising man had demanded a chance, first grabbing onto his soul in desperation, then nursing it back to health in his soft and patient ways. He was a comfort, and Mac hadn't realized how much he'd needed that, how dark his life had become until color had stumbled into it. Had given him a place to belong again.

Paris lifted his lips the rest of the way to his, the kiss he offered achingly soft and gentle, even as he yanked open the borrowed shirt, buttons flying, then shoved his hands into the back of Mac's pants, fingers clutching at his cheeks, forcing Mac to rut harder against him.

And fuck if inexperience wasn't about to bite him in the ass again, the build too good, too fast. He wasn't practiced at this, didn't know how not to go off in four seconds flat when Paris was grinding all of his hard body against him.

He ripped himself out of Paris's arms and staggered back a step, breaths heavy, climax a hair trigger from exploding. Paris's devilish grin as he lounged back against the wall wasn't helping. Neither was his hand trailing a path down his rosy red torso and into his pants, stroking his erection. With his other hand, he unbuttoned and lowered the zipper, and with no underwear on, his pants fell open to reveal his erect cock, glistening with precome.

Mac licked his lips and stumbled back a few more steps, into the corner of the table. He spread his legs as he rested back on the edge, and fuck, if his hand didn't find its way to his own cock, gliding up and down the length over the material. "Fuck, Paris, what are you doing to me?"

Paris shoved off the wall, letting his pants fall the rest of the way to floor as he sauntered toward him in nothing but a shredded shirt and suit jacket, stopping only when he was between Mac's legs, lips on his again. "Loving you." And then he was gone the next instant, before Mac could wrap his arms and legs around him, before he could show Paris how fast and hard he was falling in love with him too. As if reading his mind, Paris braced one hand on the tabletop and flipped up the tails of his shirt and coat with the other, his bare ass canted out and up. "Show me."

Mac clasped his balls and groaned. All that pale skin on display. That perfect ass that had been barely concealed in sweats the past two weeks, that as their bond had strengthened, had awakened Mac's body in ways it hadn't known for decades, waiting for him.

"Get inside me, Mac. Where you belong."

He pushed off the table and let his own pants fall. "What do I need to do? To get you ready?"

"Nothing," Paris said with a wink. "I planned ahead."

Mac cocked a brow, much to Paris's amusement, his infectious laughter filling the condo, then turning into a shivering groan as Mac skated his fingertips over the curve of his bare hip, lifting goose bumps as Mac circled behind him.

And froze.

"Fuck." The purple flared end of a plug was nestled between Paris's cheeks. The only reason Mac knew what the toy was, despite his very limited experience, was because Icarus had a habit of leaving his assortment just sitting out in the villa rooms he shared with Adam.

"You okay back there?" Paris teased.

Mac jerked his gaze up, meeting the brown one staring back at him, smoldering but also dancing with more than a little pride and mirth. The combination was as good as any dare, and while Mac usually stayed away from those, he had no intention of staying away from Paris tonight.

Stepping close, he left one hand splayed on Paris's ass while he clasped the end of the toy with the other. But as he started to pull it out, Paris shuddered and lost the tension in his arms, sinking to his elbows with a moan. Wanting more of that reaction, Mac wriggled the toy, and Paris hung his head, keening. "You like this don't you?" Same as he'd liked it the other night when Mac had stuffed him full of his fingers and made him come. He circled a fingertip around the neck of the toy, teasing Paris's rim, and Paris tried to curl his fingers into the wooden tabletop. Mac did it again, loving the way Paris's body quaked in response. "What would happen if this was my tongue instead of my finger?"

Paris shoved an arm between his body and the table, grabbing his balls as Mac had had to do earlier. When he glared back at him, his pupils were blown wide, nothing left but lust. "We can play later," he gritted out. "Please, Mac, just get inside me. I don't want to wait."

Neither did Mac; twenty-four hours was more than enough.

He shuttled his hand down his own stiff cock, spreading precome and coating his fingers, making it easier to remove the toy while still leaving a part of himself inside Paris, fascinated as Paris's hole seemed eager for more. Then losing all thought, giving himself over to sensation, as he lined up and plunged into Paris's hot and ready body.

Paris slapped the table. "Fuck, that feels good."

Even better when Mac clasped his hips and hauled Paris closer, using his grip to steady them both as he began to pound into him, over and over, his grunts twining with

Paris's pleas for more, even as his arms gave the rest of the way out and he flattened himself on the table, surrendering completely to Mac.

It was the sexiest thing Mac had ever seen. Paris splayed out in that perfect suit jacket that hugged his arms and shoulders, that accentuated his tapered back, that was flipped up so Mac could witness Paris's ass greedily taking his cock.

But Mac was greedy too, for all the things he'd never had. More pleasure, more passion, and more Paris. Bending over Paris's back, he slid his arms under his front and lifted his torso off the table, enough so he could capture Paris's lips, enough so that he sank impossibly deeper inside him, enough to taste the scream on Paris's lips as he came.

Enough to whisper "I'm loving you too" as he followed Paris over the edge.

TWENTY-FIVE

MAC STOOD in front of the floor-to-ceiling windows of Paris's bedroom, watching as the waves crested under the moonlight, listening as they broke against the sheer cliffs below. He'd been born and raised in Talahalusi; his family lived in the trees and cultivated the land. He'd spent his fair share of time in YB, but Crow Mountain with its tangled limbs and knotty roots, its trailing vines and blooming meadows was home. That said, he couldn't deny the swell of the waves, the thunder as they crashed to shore was peaceful and centering in its own way.

The bathroom light behind him flickered off, plunging the room and condo back into moonlight.

Paris's footsteps approached, then his heat wrapped around him, skin to skin, his arms circling Mac's waist as he slid in under his arm and nestled against his side, his soft cock pressed against Mac's hip. Desire tempted, but after the fast and furious release in the kitchen, then a much slower, languid one in bed, the sated want he felt for Paris was more like a warm blanket on a cold morning, a comfort. Like the ocean was to Paris. "I understand now why you keep painting it," Mac said. "Why you need it. This view is something else."

"It was the only good thing about living here." He nuzzled his pec and held him tighter. "When this is over, I don't know if I can stay in Talahalusi with you."

Mac's heart crashed like the waves below, but he couldn't say he was surprised. Someone so full of life, so bright was bound to come to his senses eventually. Of course Paris wouldn't want to be tied to him, to the duty that came with him. "I understand."

Paris's answering chuckle was a surprise, as were his words. "I don't think you do." Circling the rest of the way in front of him, Paris pushed him up against the nearest casement and cupped his cheek. "I just meant the lake isn't the same as the ocean. We may need a place near the coast too. Maybe the cabin, so long as I can drive out to the beach whenever I want."

Mac angled his face to kiss his palm. "We make it out of this . . ." Alive, together, in one piece. "I'll take you there myself. Every day."

Paris stretched up to brush their lips together, more of that soft comfort Mac had realized he liked, that Paris gave so effortlessly. He settled against his chest, fingers playing with the smattering of hair there. "I'm sorry I worried you."

"I woke up, and you weren't there." He covered Paris's hand with his, holding it over the spot where their bond hummed. "I couldn't feel you here."

"I couldn't risk it. Not until I firmed up control. And I couldn't risk Pati and her child either." He glanced away from the ocean and up at him, brown eyes searching.

"They're okay? She told Kai when they were on the phone, but I—"

"Safe and sound," Mac reassured him, carding his fingers through his hair. "And two other victims as well. You did good, Paris."

"I can do more good."

Sighing, Mac closed his eyes and leaned his forehead against the same of the too good man in his arms.

"I'm here because of you, Mac," Paris gently pressed. "You helped me find the confidence to own this, to use it for good."

"You're a target, Paris. For everyone who wants this, and for the giant who knows exactly where you are now."

Paris shivered and lowered his head, resting back against Mac's chest and looking out at the calming ocean. "It really wasn't him?"

Mac coasted a hand up and down his spine. "It was the one from the ridge."

"Why did I see the other one then?"

"He'd likely been there too. Maybe it was him when you saw them."

A beat of comfortable silence later, Paris inhaled deep and straightened in his arms, lifting his chin and meeting his gaze. "Let me do this, Mac. There's a wealth of information and connections here. We can use this for good, against the giants and Chaos."

Like Mac could argue him anything when he blazed with such confidence and conviction. But he could lay down some ground rules for the sake of safety and the bond between them. "No running off without telling me the plan."

"I'll try." Mac opened his mouth to object, but Paris's

raised hand stalled him again. "I act before I think some-times. My heart gets ahead of my head, but that's me, Mac. I'll try to be better, but I can't say I won't ever do it again. And for the record, I did have a plan yesterday morning, hours to think about it as I painted, but then I saw you asleep so soundly, and you needed it so much. I couldn't bear to wake you."

Mac lightly grasped his chin, drawing him in for a kiss, to whisper against his lips, "Next time, wake me." He drew back and brushed wavy brown strands off the pretty face that had become the center of his world. A world he had no choice but to bring Paris all the way into now. "All right, then," he said. "But if we're going to do this, we need to discuss it as part of the bigger plan, with everyone."

TWENTY-SIX

MAC WAS surprised it took Paris until they were halfway down the hall to ask, "What is this place?" Between the corner unit's boarded-up windows, the steel back door they'd entered through, and the old barrels and stacked weapons crates that crowded the hallway, it was a confusing place for any uninitiated.

Mac chuckled. "Kai asked the same thing when he first came here. It used to be a distillery tasting room. We acquired it from the lender who was going to foreclose. It serves as our base of operations here in YB since—"

"Since your father torched my house," Adam said, and Mac cut a glare his direction. He sat beside Jenn at the bar, Icarus behind it pouring vodka into shot glasses.

"No," Paris said, hand on his forearm. "That's fair. I'll make you whole," he said to Adam. "As soon as I get access to the necessary accounts."

"Don't do that," Icarus said. "Your father took a lot, from a lot of people. You'll be broke before you know it."

"Yes, but I betrayed *you*," Paris said to him, voice

earnest. "One of the few people who was good to me, so when this is done, let me help you."

The courtesan slid two shot glasses onto the bar for Adam and Jenn, then brought a third out from behind the bar and handed it to Paris. "He's loaded," he said with a head tilt toward Adam. "Being the Devil pays well. So you don't need to help us but thank you. And you were always good to me too." He pecked Paris's cheek, then flitted over to sit on the corner of the table where his sister worked on her laptop, oblivious to the mounting tension of her surroundings.

Most pointedly coming from the coyote across the room, one booted foot propped against the wall, his flannel-covered arms crossed over his broad chest. "Can we get down to business?" Robin said. "I want to know how much longer I have to be here."

"Atlas has outrun you this long," Icarus said. "How much longer are you going to keep chasing him?"

"Until I catch him."

"I told you," Mary said, not looking up from her laptop. "You'll get your turn."

"Clocks tickin', sweetheart."

Mac cleared his throat. "I don't believe you two have formally met. Robin, this is Paris. Paris, this is Robin."

Paris stepped to the center of the room, hand outstretched, and Robin, predictably, didn't move from his post on the wall. "Exactly how did you take control of your father's operation in less than twenty-four hours?"

Paris squared his shoulders and lifted his chin. "I made them an offer. I'd actually do for them what my father promised. Protection. And if they didn't want to take my offer, they could leave without retribution."

"Without even holding them? We could have questioned them."

Mac moved forward, sliding a hand into the groove of Paris's lower back, ready to intervene if he needed, but Paris seemed keen to spar with Robin.

"As I understand it from Mac," he said, "half of them were questioned already, and correct me if I'm wrong"—he split a glance between Mac and Adam—"but technically you have no authority to hold them. In fact," he leveled his gaze on Mac, "I haven't seen or heard you once mention going into the station or wherever it is you're supposed to work since you rescued me from that altar."

"They know to leave me alone this time of year."

"Sheriff's a pack member," Jenn added. "It's why he and Adam left the YB force to join the Talahalusi department."

Paris nodded, then cut a glance through all of them, eventually landing back on Robin. "I won't be my father. I won't have people working for me out of fear."

"We're all afraid right now," Robin admitted in a rare display of truth and vulnerability.

"And that's more than enough. They don't need to fear me too."

"Can we move on?" Adam said from his barstool.

"I want to know why he's after Atlas," Paris insisted, and Mac barely bit back his curse. They'd been so close to a break in hostilities, and then Paris had to go and throw a grenade into the mix.

"Because he killed my sister and brother-in-law." Robin nodded toward Adam. "His spouses."

Paris's response was immediate. "No, he didn't."

And so was Robin's, flying off the wall at him. Mac shot between them and flexed every bit of magic in him, every bit of growl in his own voice. "I love you like a brother, but if you lay a fucking paw on him, I will end you."

His eyes flashed gold, and for a second Mac feared he'd have to follow through on his promise, but then Robin thankfully backed off, his gaze sliding past Mac to Paris. "You're playing a game you don't understand, kid."

"I understand I can help," Paris said. "And that's what I intend to do."

"We have just over a week until Samhain," Mary said, reentering the conversation. She snapped shut her laptop and stood, rounding the table to prop herself next to Icarus. "The giants need to be our focus. They're the ones trying to bring through Chaos, not Atlas."

"So you say," Robin bit back.

"So I know."

"One day you're gonna spill."

"You'll be the first to know."

Robin huffed off to reclaim his spot on the wall, while brother and sister rolled their eyes. Mac almost laughed out loud. Behind him, Paris did, trying and failing to muffle it against the back of his shoulder. He didn't need to, the moment of levity easing some of the tension in the room, Mary smiling widest of all.

Mac directed Paris to the open chaise by the wall, the two of them sitting side by side, as Mary brought them up to speed. "We talked to Pati. Both giants, the one from the ridge and the one who chased you," she said to Paris, "chased her and Quinn through those tunnels."

"What about the other two giants?" Mac asked.

"No sign of them."

"I need to go to the Stick," Paris said. "If I can get one of the souls to talk, then maybe they can show me which giant was there."

"We have to be careful," Adam said. "Outside of the Canyon Lands, it's the only remaining altar site not under our control."

"And the one in La Purisima," Paris said, tossing another grenade. "I checked," he hurried on, peppering the playing field with landmines. "Dad wouldn't dare go down there himself, but he did make investments there. The only three people who can safely travel there are me and you two"—he gestured at Adam and Icarus, the only other two humans in the room—"but you both got the same look on your faces just now as Icarus's sister when I first brought it up, so I'm assuming that's a no. And I know he"—he jutted a thumb at Mac—"won't let me go, so let me send someone on Dad's—sorry, my team to check them out. "

"There's unlikely to be any Samhain activity there," Mac said. "The religious cultist won't allow it."

"Send your people," Adam said to Paris. "Assuming no activity there, then that leaves us two giants here to deal with. The one who took Paris, and one other, possibly responsible for the Stick massacre."

Paris leaned forward and propped his elbows on his knees, fully engaged in the conversation, actively partici-pating in the planning. "If we completely destroy the altar at the Stick, what happens?"

"They build a new one in its place," Adam replied. "If we don't also cleanse and secure the territory."

"And like you said, if we do that at the Stick, we'll control all of them in and around YB, other than the Canyon Lands, which I assume we'll never control?"

"Maybe the kid's not so useless," Robin said, straightening off the wall. "We could trap them."

Icarus scoffed. "Why would they be stupid enough to do that?"

"Because we have the one who got away," Robin said, his smirk bordering on feral. "The ultimate soul channeler. With Paris, they can rip the veil wide open."

"Exactly," Paris said, nodding. "I can do—"

"Absolutely not," Mac dissented, at the same time Icarus and Mary likewise expressed their objections.

"We have a week," Adam said, stepping into the fray and cutting short the debate. "Let's continue to work the case. We've got two serial killers, access to their backer's records, and a crime scene with potential witnesses." He raised his brows in question at Paris.

"I can reach them," he confirmed with a nod.

"Then let's see how far we get."

TWENTY-SEVEN

THE RISING sun did little to cut through the naturally occurring fog at the Stick. It painted Mac's windshield with a heavy, windswept mist that would've required wipers if they'd been moving instead of parked. As it were, he could barely make out Liam's raven-shaped form standing sentry on the car's hood as they waited for Jenn's advance team to confirm the giant was nowhere near the altar.

"Tell me why Robin hates Atlas so much." Paris shifted in the passenger seat, angling toward him and pulling up a leg, propping his chin on his knee. "Did Atlas really kill his sister?"

"His *twin* sister. And her husband."

"I don't follow."

Of course he didn't; he'd only heard bits and pieces of the story, usually in the midst of a heated argument. "Deborah and David were feds," Mac explained. "Adam and I were assigned as their local department contacts. Adam fell in love with them at first sight and married them a month later, conflict of interest be damned." He couldn't help but smile, remembering the Adam—then, Gabriel—of those days. Lighter, hopeful, his heart on his sleeve; a lot like Paris. After their deaths, he'd adopted the name Adam as a cover and drawn into himself, using the phoenix—his Devil —as a boogeyman against Vincent and as a shield to keep others at bay too. Until Icarus had bullied his way past the Devil and into his heart, bringing out a little more of Gabriel every day.

"Was David a coyote too?"

Mac shook his head. "David was a phoenix."

"Fuck." Paris lowered his chin, forehead on his knee, correctly anticipating the worst. "What did my father do?"

"We were building a case against him, were close to nailing him, when he sent an army after us, including Atlas. Deborah got hit with a blast of his magic." Staring out the windshield into the gray mist, Mac recalled that sunny morning ten years ago like it was yesterday. "David over-taxed himself. He was about to flame out, and he carried his wife back to the safe house where they'd left Adam. But Adam wouldn't leave them. David's flameout brought the entire structure down and started a fire that took weeks to put out. Adam was the only survivor."

Paris laid a hand on his shoulder. "I'm sorry for your loss." The warmth of his touch dissolved the knot of emotion in his throat, allowing him to tell the most critical part of the story, at least where Robin was concerned.

"Robin wasn't there when it happened. He's a merc, and he was halfway around the world on a job when Deb called the pack. He didn't answer."

"Oh shit."

Mac nodded, the sentiment spot-on. "Robin's as angry at himself as he is at Atlas."

Paris laced his hands around the front of his shin, then rested his temple on his knee, staring out the windshield. "So, if Robin wasn't there, who saw Atlas? You? Adam or Jenn? Someone else?"

"We all saw him."

"And you saw him kill Deb?"

"Me, no," Mac said. "But plenty of others did."

"I don't buy it."

"He was your father's henchman. He was in Vincent's thrall."

Paris righted his gaze, chin propped on his knee. "Then why did he make sure I had the best tutors? Why did he make sure I had the history lessons to understand the context of what's happened to me? Why did he help me help others that worked for my father? Why did he save me from my father's wrath more times than I can count?"

"Why didn't he save you that night we did?"

Paris lowered his knee and raked a hand through his hair, tugging at the ends, frustration bubbling over. "It doesn't add up, Mac."

Mac knew the feeling well. "For the record," he said, "I don't disagree with you." Paris whipped his gaze back to him. "He helped us save Adam and Icarus the night your father was killed. And she knows something she's not telling anyone, about Atlas and all this."

"Maybe you should trust her."

Blind trust didn't come easy, though. Not for a cop and not for someone who'd witnessed allegiances shift and sway through the years. She was Nature, the highest power in their world, but to what end she used that power, and how she moved them all around her chessboard in her game with Chaos, was still a mystery. As someone who solved those for a living, Mac didn't like being kept in the dark. And as someone who found himself miraculously bonded again, falling more in love with the person—the human—in the car beside him each day, he liked it even less. He had too much at stake now; he needed to know the rules and the players, all of them.

His phone beeped with a text, interrupting his darkening thoughts. He read the text from Jenn aloud. "All clear." Paris inhaled deep and straightened in his seat, steeling himself, but the fear in his eyes was unmistakable. Mac cupped the side of his neck. "You don't have to do this."

"I want to," he replied with zero hesitation.

Fuck, he was amazing. Mac hadn't been bluffing when he'd told Robin he'd end him if he laid a hand on Paris. He would go to war for this man, against anyone. He drew Paris closer and kissed him deep, pouring all his affection into the kiss and their bond. "Then I'm with you every step of the way." Exiting the car, they met at the edge of the sandy path that snaked through the sea grass. Mac laced their fingers together, giving Paris's a squeeze. "I didn't get to say it before, but I'm proud of you. For making a stand, for the way you handled your father's assets, and for the way you handled Robin."

"I could do that because of you. My father snuffed it out all my life, but you helped bring it back. Bring me back." Paris returned the earlier kiss, and then they followed Liam's lead through the fog, wind whipping the sea grass and fog around them, soaking them through by the time they reached the clearing where Jenn and Abigail waited. The pack had spread out along the peninsula's land edges, while Liam and the flock of corvids were scattered along the rocky beach behind the remnants of the giant's altar.

As Paris gravitated toward the altar, Mac surveyed the rest of the scene. The charred mounds of flesh and bone in a semicircle, the burnt sea grass around the edges of the scene, the deep stains in the earth. All familiar, reminding him of the ridge, except for the silence.

He joined Paris by the altar, a broken mess of rock and driftwood, the pile of bones from the picture Mary had received gone. "A reaper's been here already," Mac said, and Paris nodded.

But as Paris stepped around the altar, he froze midstride and swung his wide-eyed gaze back to Mac. "Out there," he said with a nod toward the Bay, and as Mac drew closer, he heard it too, a whisper on the edge of the waves.

Paris took off running, scattering crows and ravens as he tripped and slipped over slick rocks. Mac grabbed the back of his jacket, helping him stay upright, but as they hit the edge of the water, there was no stopping Paris from sinking to his knees and plunging his hands into the cold, dark water.

Liam jumped into the air, squawking in alarm.

"I know," Mac said. "I know." His worry ratcheted higher with each passing second, the water lapping at their knees too cold for Paris to withstand, but he was gone from his plane, lost in whatever vision the voice on the waves was sharing with him. In human form, the best Mac could do was curl around his body and keep him warm, then be there for him when he returned.

Which he did after another minute, shivering and pale, and with a purple hue to his brown eyes. Mac gasped. What was happening to him? But before that question could occupy more of his thoughts, Paris stuttered through chattering teeth, "I saw him. The giant who did this."

Mac bundled him in his arms and lifted him out of the water, Jenn and Abigail steadying him as he crossed the rocks back to stable ground. "Can you paint him?"

"I don't need to," Paris said, voice fraught with agony—and terror. "I know who he is."

Mac stumbled. Would've hit the dirt if not for Jenn and Abigail holding them up. "How?"

"He worked for my father."

TWENTY-EIGHT

MAC STOOD at the end of the island in his parents' bustling, chaotic kitchen, unsure if he'd made the right decision fleeing his place for the evening to come here. But he'd been shooed out of the infirmary by Monte and Chaz, and he hadn't wanted to stay on the main floor either, listening through the ceiling as Icarus streamed a scene, Adam watched him, and the inevitable ensued. Maybe Mary could tune that out with her headphones and hacking, but he'd nearly died of embarrassment the first time, no doubt would for sure now that he had a better idea of what exactly was going on upstairs. Pati likewise wasn't there to distract him, the elders and midwives from her tribe having made the journey to the mountain and set up camp on one of the outparcels. Not far from where Robin and Jenn were meeting with the rest of the pack to organize the hunt for Wallace Boyle, the giant Paris had identified from his vision at the Stick.

"No Paris tonight?" Rena asked, as if reading his mind.

She sat between Cherry and Abernathy at the kitchen's eat-in table, helping the children ice a cake.

"He's in YB with Abigail, Jason, and Kai. Recon for her." Once they'd had a face and name to go with another giant on their map, the search was on. Mac had held Paris through the rest of the day and night, made sure he'd recovered from his dip in the cold Bay, and then reluctantly seen him off yesterday morning to the condo in YB. He would have liked to keep him at home another day, to wallow in the bond between them before it disappeared again, but Paris's drive to do something was irrepressible. "They'll be back later tonight."

"Yay!" Cherry and Abernathy cheered, spatulas in the air, icing more of the table than the cake.

"When do we get to meet this man?" his mom asked as she slid the foil-covered skillet of ratatouille he'd helped assemble into the oven. Normally, he stayed out of the way, but he'd gotten used to cooking with Paris. "The kids can't stop talking about him." She wiped her hands on the front of her apron, then slipped it off over her head, her silver and black braid resettling over her shoulder. "I didn't think anyone could top Icarus as their favorite."

"You should bring him to the Samhain festival," his dad said from where he and Liam were slathering loaves of bread with garlic butter.

"I wanted to talk to you about that," Mac started, only to be cut off by his youngest brother, Declan, who joined Rena and the kids at the table, taking a swipe of icing for himself.

"It's dangerous, thin veil, we know the drill, brother."

"This is different," Mac insisted. "The giants are going to try and open it this year. All the way."

"They try every year."

"This is *different*." His family took their role as stewards of the land and souls seriously, but he needed them to understand that it was beyond serious this time. That Chaos was pressing harder and was closer than ever.

"He's not exaggerating," Liam said. "What we've seen this past month . . ." He shook his head. "We haven't had a fight like this on our hands since the Rift."

"Which we lost ground in," Mac said. "We're more powerful this time, but so is Chaos."

His mother came around the island and pushed between them, her arms around their waists, hugging them both. "We'll keep it small, then. Only family and folks who work with us here."

"Mom."

"It's tradition." Mostly from his father's Gaelic roots, but his mother's people also celebrated, giving thanks for the harvest and honoring the souls they'd delivered. "But we will also stand guard, over our harvest, our plane, and our family."

Mac could live with that compromise. He dropped a kiss on the crown of her head. "Thank you," he said. "I can't go into this worrying about you and also having to protect him."

She tipped her head back, her dark brows waggling. He'd opened the door with a slip of his words, and she wasn't going to let it go this time.

"You might as well tell them," Rena said. "They know."

"Know what?" Declan said.

"That you've bonded again," his father replied as he tucked the garlic bread into the other oven. "We know."

"How?" Mac gasped.

"One, you're in the kitchen cooking," Rena said.

"I missed—"

"Cooking with him?" Liam said with a knowing smile.

His mother grinned up at him. "Just because we no longer deliver the souls doesn't mean we can't hear them. Especially when they sing."

"I didn't want to tell you, in case—"

"In case what happens with Hank happens again." She let go of Liam so she could turn fully to him, hugging him tight. "I'm happy for you, son."

"But I don't think I'll survive it when my other half is torn away again." Paris was still on his list; there was no erasing or taking that back. And he'd gone and made himself seen, a blinking target for the giants and for anyone who wanted a piece of his father's empire. He was the center of the storm—and of Mac's world.

His mother patted his chest, over the spot where his bond with Paris lived. "When the time comes, your soul will get what it deserves."

"What does that mean?"

"We didn't just retire, son," his father said. "My name appeared on your mother's list."

Mac jolted, having to use his mother to catch his wavering weight. "What?" He'd been told his parents chose to retire, that they'd handed him the reaper title because they'd decided to create life rather than ferry it elsewhere.

Not this.

How had they even survived?

His mother shuffled him to the stool beside his father, the two of them making sure he was steady. Good thing as she continued to deliver blow after blow. "Nature came to us and gave us a choice. We'd done enough. She'll give you the same choice."

"Why didn't I get a choice last time?" he asked, voice cracking with pain and regret, all of it washing back up, a tsunami of memories. Hank's name appearing, the bond between them fraying, then later that same night, a phone call asking him to come identify a body. Hank's lifeless frame in the morgue, in his arms, the bond between them severed for good as he'd taken Hank's soul across the veil, delivering it to the peace it deserved. He'd never known pain like that day before or since. Had cast love aside, never wanting to feel that sort of agony again, until Paris Cirillo had grabbed hold and made him his.

"Because the last time it wasn't about you," his father said. "Your aura then versus now . . ." His dark eyes glittered, a sprinkling of the green magic from his mother's maternal line, some of their coven's gifts passing to him too. "It's completely changed. Before, it was red in the center, with blue and violet around the outside, but now . . . Now you feel everything, blue and violet, the red bleeding through from the outside, and at the center, green. Your connection to Nature wasn't there before. You've changed."

"He's right," Liam said. "And not just because of Paris."

"Nature needed you," his mom said. "You've delivered her two phoenixes, a white raven, an eagle, and now a medium. You're her warrior, and for that loyalty, she'll give you and Paris what your souls deserve, same as she did ours."

———

It was past midnight when Mac returned to his thankfully quiet house, only the muffled beep of monitors drifting up from the infirmary below.

Dinner at the main house had been good, the dessert a sticky delicious mess and the Samhain planning afterward reassuring. His family had heard what he and Liam had said and were taking the situation seriously, even Declan. They'd have their celebration, but by keeping it small, they could better protect the gathered people, including Pati and her tribe, and once they were secure, provide support to neighboring farms as needed. Mac didn't want them stretched too thin, especially if he, Adam, and the rest of the pack leaders were dealing with the giants elsewhere.

Especially if Paris remained in his family's protection here. Paris would no doubt object, and if he and Adam needed him on the scene, then that was where he'd be. But if not, if he stayed behind here, Mac wanted him safe. Because after what his parents had told him, for the first time since Paris had grabbed hold of his soul—hell, since he'd lost Hank—he saw an alternative to heartache and loneliness in his future. A spark of hope—of love—that might grow into the kind of roaring blaze Paris had loved to build in the hearth back at the cabin.

Granted, part of him was still angry that he'd been denied the chance with Hank, but Nature's mysteries had been coming hard and fast lately, and as he stood in the doorway of his bedroom, taking in a slumbering Paris in the moonlight, he couldn't deny he was thankful for the opportunity to get to know this amazing man.

To love him.

He also couldn't deny that in this moment he understood Paris's instinct the other morning to leave him asleep in the bed. He looked so peaceful, the steady rise and fall of his tapered back, his dark hair tousled against the white sheets. After two very long days of digging into his father's dealings, Paris had left his precious ocean to come back to Monte Corvo, back to him. He should let him sleep.

Turning for his office, he barely made it a step when "Come to bed, Mac," rumbled from behind him.

He glanced over his shoulder. Paris was still on his stomach, the sheets tangled around his waist, but his breaths weren't as long and steady as before. Mac felt guilty for disturbing his rest. "I can let you—"

"You need to sleep too," Paris mumbled into the pillow. "Get in bed."

Smiling at the gentle, muffled order, Mac undressed and crawled in beside him, soaking in the warmth and trailing a hand down his spine, savoring the goose bumps that rose in his wake. "Everything good in YB?"

"Got what we needed." Paris scooted more fully into the curve of him, hitching up a leg so Mac could line his up behind it, nestling them closer. "What'd you have for dinner?"

"Ratatouille."

Mac couldn't see his smile, Paris's face angled away, but he could hear it in his sleepy voice. "Can never spell that right on the first try."

Mac muffled his laughter, his love in Paris's shoulder. What had he done without this light, this warmth in his life for so long?

"You had a good night?" Paris asked once Mac's laughter subsided.

"I learned a lot." That maybe he could keep this light, this warmth, this incredible man for longer than his list prescribed. He trailed his fingers along his back, telling Paris exactly how he felt, Paris's breaths evening out more with each letter Mac brushed over his skin, from the I to the L-O-V-E to the U. Mac stretched an arm across his back, rested his cheek against his shoulder, and closed his eyes. "I learned that maybe I can keep you. Forever."

Paris's reply reached him on the edge of sleep, on the terrifying, wonderful edge of hope. "I love you too."

TWENTY-NINE

THE PEACEFUL REPRIEVE lasted barely a day. Paris's momentum inside his father's organization was halted by a freeze on the Cirillo funds. Mary had traced the action to Charlotte Taylor, Vincent's human accountant. Mac had a file on her already; she'd been cooking the books for Vincent for years, moving his money around to keep it sheltered. If anyone had the inside track on where Vincent's money was and how to tie it up, it was Charlotte.

It had taken another day to arrange a meet. Mac was against it, suspecting a trap. Mary would eventually hack through the wall. But Adam, the traitor, had sided with Paris in the no-time-to-waste camp. Which was how they found themselves in a back office at Club Sutro, a relatively neutral site, and thanks to Kai's and Icarus's connections, one they were able to access in the middle of the afternoon, limiting collateral damage if things went sideways. Which they always did.

Paris seemed to sense that, his loafers wearing a hole in

the carpet at the far end of the room where he paced. Adam, Icarus, and Robin were more comfortable with the inevitable chaos, lounging around a table in the corner, topping up their caffeine, while Mary sat behind the desk, furiously typing on her laptop.

Mac pushed off the front of the desk and crossed the room, making a barrier of himself in Paris's pacing circle. "You don't have to do this," he told him, as he smoothed down the lapels of his suit jacket. "We can send Adam out to negotiate."

"The Devil?" Paris scoffed. "You know that's what they still call him, right? They'll think *we're* trying to trap *them*."

Robin set aside his mug. "I fail to see the problem."

Paris's jaw clenched, and Mac bit back a laugh. Robin worked everyone's last nerve, even Paris's. "Look," he said, stepping around Mac to address the table. "Folks are on edge. They know I'm working with you. They also need to know there won't be reprisals."

"She's also holding your accounts hostage," Adam said.

"Which is the trap they won't see coming," Paris said, then asked Mary, "How long do you need?"

"Ten minutes," she replied.

"Question is," Robin mused, "do you want the money for yourself or for the cause?"

"Which is it, Robin?" Paris snapped, irritated to outburst. "You don't believe me because we thought they'd all fallen in line? Or because they didn't?"

"Hey," Mac said, stepping between them and cupping Paris's cheek, waiting for his brown gaze to settle back on his. "I know it feels like he's the enemy, but he's not."

"We've all been there," Icarus said, earning a growl from

Robin. Which in turn earned a raspberry from Icarus. And like a popped balloon, the tension in the room deflated, everyone except Robin chuckling.

Paris inhaled deep, then exhaled, letting more of the tension go as he shook out his shoulders. When he righted his gaze, he was calm once more, confident, the spat with Robin doing some good it seemed. "We've seen it already. When we talk to people, when we let them be heard, we get more information out of them. We add allies. We learn how to win this." He nodded. "I can do this."

Mac was sure of it. Sure of him. And sure that if he didn't kiss him right then, he'd regret it. In front of everyone, he pulled the man he loved into his arms and kissed him deep, hoping Paris sensed all the pride and confidence Mac had in him. To pull this off, to pull anything off he set his mind to.

Paris kissed him back, his lips curving into a smile against his, the two of them parting when cat calls and whistles erupted. In his arms, Paris laughed with the joy, the warmth that had brightened Mac's world these past few weeks. And more, according to Paris. "You should see your aura right now," he whispered at his year. "I can't wait to get home so I can paint it. So you can see it too."

Mac couldn't wait either.

And neither could reality, interrupting the happy moment. "Eyes on Taylor," Mary said.

Lounging ceased. Adam and Robin shot to their feet, Icarus too, the latter coming around the table to hook his arm through Paris's. The both of them were stylishly suited, though Icarus stood several inches taller in his stilettos. "You ready to go?"

Paris would meet Charlotte with Icarus, their best fighter, at his side. Jason was already in the main room, behind the bar with Kai, and Adam, Robin and Mac would join them, fanned out to block the exit doors. Jenn and Abigail would shift from their positions on the floor to the room here with Mary, as guards and backup.

"Last line of human defense," Paris said with a sharp nod, then tucked the folders Mac handed him under his arm. Ammunition, for when he needed it. One last stolen kiss, and then their group strode down the hall to the main room, Paris and Icarus continuing to the lone table in the center of the dance floor where Charlotte Taylor waited, two men—shifters they'd already identified as her usual entourage—standing guard behind her.

"This is the company you keep now?" she said, her dainty nose turned up, her brown hair twisted in a bun at her neck.

"This was always the company I kept." Paris lowered into the chair Icarus pulled out for him and set the folders on the table. "You're holding my money hostage."

"Your money?" She scoffed. "You think you should be the heir? A worthless layabout who stole from his own father? You don't know the first thing about running a business."

"So you want the money for yourself, then?"

"We're the ones who earned it."

We, Mac noted. As in the royal *we*, or the *we* that included the two shifters behind her, or a larger *we* of more defectors?

Didn't matter for Paris's response, though, the strategy planned. "You're right," he said, and Charlotte reared back, her eyes wide with surprise. "I don't know how to run the finances," he said to her, then to the two shifters and whomever they were also standing in for, "And I wasn't the one my father sent into battle. So no, I don't know how to run his business, as he did. I'll need your help, *all* of you, to run it a different way."

"And how's that?" she asked, leaning slightly forward, giving away the interest she hid behind her skepticism.

"The way my father should have. By affording you the protection you came to him for in the first place." He opened one of the folders, pushing it toward her, and Charlotte paled. "You came to my father for protection for your daughter, a witch who inherited your late husband's magic. What did Vincent make her do instead?"

She hesitated, fingers splayed on the edge of the picture of her daughter.

"He's gone, Charlotte," Paris said. "My father can't hurt your family anymore. Let me help you. Let me help her."

"Potions," she said after another moment. "Killing ones. They've made her sick too."

"And you, Frankie," Paris said, as he glanced up at the blond shifter behind her. "You're a psychopomp. You should be delivering souls to peace, not to the highest bidder." He opened a different folder. "My father found you and offered you protection from a gang who sought to kill you instead of having their souls delivered. What did my father have you do instead?"

He cast his hazel gaze aside. "Deliver them to a giant." Wallace Boyle, if Mac had to guess, another reason Paris had lobbied for recruiting Charlotte and her guards.

"I won't do that," Paris said, conviction and earnestness in his voice. "I'll give you the protection he promised."

"And if we disagree?" the other shifter asked.

"You leave here unharmed."

"And your money?" Charlotte said.

"Is mine now, regardless."

She cursed, then snatched her phone out of her purse, tapping the screen a few times before glancing back at him with an incredulous glare. "This was a trap."

"To free my money, yes, but the offer to free you is also very real."

Through it all, Paris had kept his voice even, calm, gentle almost. No smirk, no victory smile, just the caring, empathetic human who was offering a lifeline, and Charlotte, Mac was sure, was ready to take it, but then Frankie said, "It's too late."

She whirled around in her chair. "What do you mean it's too late? This is a good deal. Better than the other one."

Icarus had shifted forward, muscles coiled. "What other one?"

"I thought it was a trap." Frankie's hazel eyes shifted from Icarus to where Jason had hopped the bar, then to each of Robin's, Adam's, and Mac's positions, all of them moving closer. "I already said yes."

"You were supposed to wait!" Charlotte yelled.

But her bellow was barely audible over the sound of metal ripping apart above, an opening torn in the roof, followed by a rain of fireballs.

Paris yanked on the bond, and Mac's gaze collided with his frightened one. Only a second before Icarus covered his head and hauled him out of the chair, dragging him back toward the bar where Jason stood churning out fireballs of his own.

Mac mentally calculated how fast he could reach them, by foot or wing, but then his math was rearranged by

Wallace Boyle falling through the hole in the roof, the giant's feet hitting the floor with a massive rumble. A firefight ensued, cutting off Mac's path, as Jason and Wallace exchanged shots, the latter's height and breadth growing by the second, the tattoos on his skin coming to life, weapons and beasts on the cusp of materializing into this reality.

"Where's the medium?" he bellowed.

A shifted Robin launched at the giant, aiming for his knees, while Adam aimed a shot at his head. Neither attack landed, Wallace deftly maneuvering out of the way—toward where Icarus stood over Kai, Paris, and Charlotte behind a wall of fire Jason had erected. A wall the giant would likely walk right through if Mac didn't do something.

He didn't have a clear path himself, not one that wouldn't push the giant closer to the vulnerable, but he did have a clear path to call in reinforcements so that he, Robin, and Adam could get a better shot at Wallace.

Arms raised, tapping into the two ancient magics that ran through his veins, he recited the words of his ancestors, calling down the wind. And on the next gust that blew through the opening in the roof, Liam led a wave of ravens and crows, all of them flying at the giant's head, disorienting him and causing him to stagger back a step.

Almost enough for Robin to take him down, for Adam to take another shot.

"Seasamh síos!"

Mac went down on one knee, the order issued with power, with magic greater than his own, and the rest of the corvids obeyed too, falling away from the giant, whose gaze locked once more on Paris.

Mac swung his own gaze the direction of the call, to the

top of the bar where a certain missing warlock stood wielding a crossbow.

"Stay down!" Atlas yelled for everyone else's benefit.

Right before he unleashed a bronze arrow that sailed through the air and into Wallace Boyle's chest, putting an end to another giant.

THIRTY

"IS THIS REALLY NECESSARY?" Paris gestured at the caged corner of the basement barrel room where Mac's family kept a collection of library wines . . . and today, a warlock of dubious intent.

"It's for his protection more than ours," Mac said with a pointed look across the room to Robin seething in a club chair, thinly veiled hate swirling in his golden eyes. The only reason they'd made it back to Talahalusi with Atlas in one piece was because Adam had forced Robin to make the trip on paw to "run the murderous impulses out." Mac didn't think it had worked.

For his part, Atlas didn't seem the least bit fazed, resting back against a barrel and magically stitching together a tear in his kilt. Otherwise, the warlock looked his usual put-together self, not a blond hair out of place, his green eyes bright, his thin black tee hugging his fit, compact torso. Sounded like his usual acerbic self too. "One, I can snap my fingers and be out of here whenever I want." He finished with his kilt and straightened, perusing the shelves of wine behind him. "And two," he said as he withdrew a bottle Mac recognized well, "if memory serves, this vintage had a perfect rating and trades in the high six figures." He was right on both counts, and when he sizzled through the wax and cork and drank straight from the bottle, Mac had to tamp down his own murderous impulses.

Paris did his part to calm him too, turning his back on Atlas and patting Mac's chest, those big brown eyes gazing up at him. "He's an ass, but he saved my life."

"About that . . ." Robin said. "You two been working together the entire time?"

Atlas laughed out loud. "No, and truth be told, I'm amazed he's managed to stay alive this long."

Paris spun around so fast he almost stumbled, Mac's arm around his waist the only thing that held him upright. The loss of balance didn't stop his "Hey!" from sounding any less indignant. "What about all those tutors? All those books you made me read? You prepared me for this. If I'd failed, it would've been your fucking fault."

Atlas shrugged and took another slug from the bottle before wiping his mouth on his leather gauntlet. "I did what I could, but you still made some questionable choices." His green gaze slid toward Icarus, who, sitting on Adam's lap at the table across from Robin, flipped him the middle finger.

Mac was on the verge of screaming *Children!* when Paris laid a hand over his on his waist, refocusing Mac on the matter at hand—what role had Atlas played in another giant coming after Paris today? More than timely savior? Robin was right to question.

"Why are you here?" Mac asked.

"Because I got wind you"—he nodded at Paris—"had

sent some of Vincent's soldiers to look for the giant in La Purisima."

Robin pushed out of his chair and strolled closer to the cage. "You buddies?"

"Don't think so, seeing as I put a bolt in his chest too."

Adam bumped Icarus off his lap and stood too, joining Robin in front of the cage. "So it's just the one who tried to kill Paris left?"

"Like he wants it to be. He wants to do it himself. Your father," he said to Paris, "wanted to be Chaos's right hand. The giant wanted to be Chaos's champion."

Mac instinctively drew Paris closer, tightening his hold. "Then why did you hand Paris over to him?"

"Because I was trying to find out who he is. He's erased. Vincent always talked about him as a partner but never by name. I would have found out that night, tracked him down and killed him, if all of you hadn't interfered."

Paris shivered in his arms. "I could have died."

"The sacrifice would've been worth it."

Only Paris in his arms kept Mac from flying at the cage. Icarus, though, did it for him, growling as he wrapped his hands around the iron bars. Atlas lifted a hand, like he was about to snap himself out of near death, but then Mary stepped out of the shadows and laid a hand on her brother's shoulder, backing him off while her gaze remained locked on the warlock. "That wouldn't have made me happy," she said to Atlas.

He sneered . . . but tellingly rocked back a step on his leather knee-high boots. "Unlike others, *I* don't take orders from you." He tipped back the bottle and took an even healthier gulp.

"But you sent me that footage from the Stick, didn't you? Were they both there?"

"Only Wallace. I needed to try to draw him out again."

Paris's shivers turned to vibrations, a rare flash of anger riding a wave of hurt. He pushed out of Mac's hold, shoved himself between Icarus and Mary, and stared Atlas down through the bars. "So you used me as bait. Again."

"I won't say I'm sorry. That's one less giant we have to deal with."

"I defended you to them."

He tipped back the bottle one last time, then tossed the empty aside, the glass shattering against the concrete floor. "Don't bother." And with a snap, he was gone.

———

Mac found Paris upstairs in the kitchen, head in the fridge, yanking out ingredients and tossing them onto the island behind him. Seemingly at random: mushrooms, yogurt, onion, cilantro. Afraid of what might come next, Mac hustled across the room and pushed the fridge door closed, forcing Paris out, but not before he'd snatched another carton of mushrooms.

"I'm gonna cook," he sniffled, spinning toward the island as he swiped at the tears on his cheeks.

"No," Mac said, curling an arm around his waist and drawing him into his arms. "You're gonna breathe." He gently tugged at the carton of mushrooms in Paris's hand. "And you're going to let these go because in no world do they belong with the rest of those ingredients."

"I was going to make dill sauce," he said as he released his hostage mushrooms.

"With cilantro?"

His gaze shot to the island, eyes widening. "Fuck, that's gross."

"Very." Mac chuckled, tossed the extra mushrooms aside, and pulled Paris the rest of the way into his arms, gliding a hand up and down his back until his breathing calmed and his tears subsided. "You good?"

"Debatable." A heavy sigh later, he took a half step out of his arms, resting back against the island. "I know I volunteered to be bait a few days ago, but that was on my terms. He used me. Twice!"

"Atlas always has his own agenda."

"I just . . ."

"You just what?"

"Want to be respected," he said with a shrug, casting his gaze aside.

Mac closed the distance between them once again, physically and through their bond, sending admiration and affection through it. Finger curled under Paris's chin, he lifted his face and stared into his eyes, wanting Paris to see —to believe—the truth in his. "I respect you. You are smart, caring, and *good*."

A beautiful blush warmed his pale cheeks, heat flickering in his eyes too. "You're not exactly impartial."

He didn't take the tempting bait. Gliding his hand lower, he cupped the side of Paris's neck. "Everyone here respects you."

"Except Robin."

"Robin doesn't respect anyone."

Paris's watery laugh under his palm felt like victory. He wanted more of those laughs—Paris needed more of those laughs after the day he'd had—and Mac knew just where to get them.

"Put the stuff back in the fridge," he told Paris.

"I was going to make us dinner. I'll find not gross stuff."

Mac shook his head. "There's something else I want to do instead."

"What's that?"

"Introduce you to my parents."

———

Adam and Icarus had graciously surrendered their meadow for the family Samhain gathering. A pavilion stood in the middle of the clearing, round tables and chairs scattered underneath, a long buffet table at one end that in a few days would be overflowing with the bounty of their harvest. Mac leaned against a pole, eavesdropping as his mother animatedly explained to Paris how everything would be set up, what all would be served. Paris oohed and aahed in all the right places, asking about recipes and offering some of his own. All of it genuine, his mother taking to him right away, and when the topic of bread came up, Paris won a mega fan in his father too. Just as Mac had suspected he would. Same as Paris had won Liam over from the start, then Rena and the kids; even Declan had warmed up to him over the past hour as they'd helped with the setup.

Because as Mac had told Paris in the kitchen, he was good. Caring and smart, a kind soul who was loyal to his friends, who'd made sure they were protected, who still carried guilt over the one he'd betrayed, and who'd helped save the pregnant then-stranger now laughing at a table with Mary and Kai. Even if Mac had saved Paris's soul out of some selfish instinct, it had been the right call, because he hadn't truly known then what Paris's soul deserved. Not like he did now.

"You're in love with him," Adam said, the truth not startling, nor the man, his footsteps heavier now that he was human again. He leaned against the next pole over, arms crossed, gaze tracking Icarus as he and Jason chased Cherry and Abernathy around the tables with the gingham cloths they were supposed to be spreading on each, not trying to wrap the kids up in them.

"I'm sorry I doubted you," Mac said. "When you told me how you felt about Icarus. I get it now."

"In fairness, you took a few days longer."

Mac shook his head, a small resigned smile—fate—making his lips curve. "He grabbed hold that night at the altar, and I didn't deliver him."

Gasping, Adam shot off the pole. "He's on your list?"

"Has been since that night."

Adam clasped his shoulder. "Mac—"

"There may be a way around it," he said, cutting off the sympathy that threatened in his friend's voice. He didn't need condolences. He needed a miracle, the same kind that had held his family together once before. "My father was on my mother's list. That's the real reason they retired."

Adam's gaze drifted back out under the tent, to where Paris stood chatting with his parents. "They're still here. Happy and healthy."

Mac's attention drifted elsewhere, to his brother snatching up his kids midrun, hauling them under his arms, all of them laughing, free and easy, unburdened. His gut churned. "I don't know if I can do it to him."

"Liam wants it, Mac. He's ready."

"But Rena and the kids . . ."

"Will keep him grounded. And when it's Declan's turn or one of the kids', it'll pass to them. No one expects you to do this forever, except you."

He swung his gaze back to Adam. "So Paris and I just go off to our happily ever after?"

Adam chuckled. "You two would fail at that as badly as me and Icarus. Paris has a gift, and so do you, as a detective and as a raven with acute observation skills. Those won't go away just because you give up the reaper. And we'll all help Liam because that's what family does." He squeezed his shoulder and gifted Mac one of his rare smiles, though thanks to Icarus, they were coming more frequently again these days.

Mac hated to wipe it from his face, but he had one more favor to ask, and Adam was the only person he trusted to fulfill it. "If for some reason he doesn't make it, I don't want to either. Not again."

Using the hand still on his shoulder, Adam pulled him into a crushing embrace. "I hope it doesn't come to that, but if it does, you have my word."

Mac hugged him back, blinking back tears and forcing words out around the lump in his throat. "Thank you."

"Hey, wallflowers!" Icarus shouted, yanking them out of their melancholy moment. They drew apart, eyeing the courtesan standing with Paris mid-tent, the former holding up an orange gingham, Paris a violet one. "Need your votes."

Paris's smile grew wider with each step Mac came closer, his gaze bright with happiness, with the confidence Atlas and Robin had tried unsuccessfully to chip away at, with the love that had been growing between them these past few weeks, that Mac had no intention of existing without.

"I like the violet," he said as Mac reached him.

"I should hope so." Smirking, he looped an arm around Paris's waist, trapping him in said violet and kissing him with his whole soul.

Cheers erupted and a camera clicked somewhere, capturing the second love of his life. His last. "Forever," he whispered against Paris's lips.

"Forever," his mate promised back.

THIRTY-ONE

INFIRMARY NO LONGER NEEDED, the tasting table had been moved back into the barrel room and all but one seat was occupied around it, the room full of people, including Mac with Paris sitting beside him, waiting for the last person to arrive.

To confirm the wheels had been set in motion.

Jason, on the other side of Paris, leaned across the table, asking Icarus, "What happened to Miss Types-Like-the-Wind?"

"You wouldn't want me to send these messages to the wrong people, would you?" Mary said as she cleared the bottom step.

No, they would not. With Charlotte's help decoding Vincent's books and contacts, Mac's cold case files and access to missing persons reports, the pack digging deeper into Atlas's potential whereabouts, and Mary hacking surgical records, official and not, they'd identified three possible suspects as the giant who'd attacked Paris, all of them erased persons, presumably all the names they'd associated with them aliases too.

Brett Barrett.

Samuel Thomas.

Neil Roberts.

And just now, Mary had sent encrypted emails to each, putting it out there that Paris, as Vincent's successor, wanted to meet at the Stick tomorrow, the day before Samhain, to discuss a possible partnership for future endeavors. They were counting on the giant, whichever one he was, to see an opportunity he couldn't pass up. A chance to catch the one who got away.

And Paris acting the bait on his own terms, with plenty of backup.

Mac looked again at the pictures of their three suspects —a single photo of each that Mary had managed to scrounge up. "Can you give us a more likely than not?" he asked Paris.

Paris pulled each photo closer, taking a long look then trading one for another. "All of them are the right build and appearance, perfectly average. But all of their beards are too thick for me to see if the scar is there," he said, tapping at the spot on Brett's chin where the raised slash would be. "And the photos are too grainy to see much else."

"Best I could find," Mary said. "We're lucky to get any for erased persons."

"Samuel is the most likely candidate," Robin said. "If that report he paid a surgeon for fixing his face after a bar fight is legit."

"A bar that has the ingredients for the drink you smelled on his breath," Mac said.

"Wrong eye color," Jenn countered.

"Could be contacts," Kai said, and he would know. The white raven's contacts had fooled people for years into thinking he was a human.

"Then there's the loan shark, Neil," Abigail said. "Vincent did business with him."

"He could've taken that knife Paris painted as collateral," Jason speculated. "High value." The smuggler would know.

But Icarus shook his head. "Atlas would've known him."

"That might be an apron Brett is wearing," Liam said, peering at the photo he'd snagged from in front of Paris.

"Store clerk, janitor, mechanic would make sense for an erased person," Adam said. "He bounces around, gets paid under the table."

Paris shoved back from the table with a frustrated grunt. "*If, might, could be* . . . We don't know anything for sure," he said, raking his hands through his hair as he paced away from the table.

Mac rose slowly, not cutting him off abruptly this time, but letting Paris wind down as he circled back to where Mac stood. When he was in front of him, Mac laid a hand over his stomach. "Who do you think it is *here*, in your gut?"

"It could be any of—"

He splayed his fingers. "Who, Paris?"

"Brett," he answered without hesitation. "Adam is right, and the malice in his eyes . . . Whomever he was looking at, he hated them. That was the way he looked at Lola." His whole body shivered, and Mac wrapped an arm around his shoulders while the remembered fear passed.

"Brett is priority one," he told the group over his shoulder. "But we still need to be ready for Samuel or Neil."

"If we can find them," Mary said. "I'll keep digging, but no known addresses as of yet."

"What if I'm wrong?" Paris said, quietly, as if intended only for Mac's ears, but in a room full of shifters and magical beings, everyone heard him.

And of course Robin was the one to press, the coyote strolling over to where they stood. "You can't go into this and be knocked off your game if it's not Brett who shows up at the Stick tomorrow."

He was an asshole, but he wasn't wrong. Given the geography of the location, the plan depended on Paris keeping the giant, whomever he turned out to be, talking long enough to one, incriminate himself, and two, allow the teams to converge from the water, air, and land.

The asshole, it seemed, tended to bring out the fight in Paris. He straightened his spine and lifted his chin, glaring Robin down. "As long as you're on your game to catch the fucker."

Behind them, Icarus and Jason high-fived, and Robin even cracked a smirk. "We'll be ready," he said, then gestured to the table. "Let's go over those mission specs one more time so you'll know exactly where we're coming from."

With a nod, Paris led them back to the table, and after another hour of planning, the meeting broke up, folks scattering for the evening.

Paris moved to stand too, but Mac placed a hand on his knee, holding him seated until it was just the two of them left in the room. He rotated Paris in his chair toward him, their knees bumping. "It's just me now," he said. "I know you can do this, I believe in you, but if you have any doubt, or if you don't want to do this, you always have an out." They were asking a lot of someone who was relatively new to this war, who hadn't been fighting it for decades like him and many of the others. "You just have to tell me."

Paris shook his head, sharp and certain. "I'm the last line of human defense," he said, repeating the mantra he'd said to Icarus the other day. "We need a place in this fight. This is our home too. I intend to defend it."

"All right," Mac said, standing and offering Paris his hand. "Tomorrow we fight. But tonight, I have something else in mind."

THIRTY-TWO

MAC HAD BEEN SNEAKING glances every so often at Paris in the passenger seat, watching his smile grow wider as he grew more certain of their destination. He was beaming by the time Mac pulled his car into the drive at the cabin in Calera.

Paris climbed out, inhaled deep, then spun, asking him over the car roof, "What are we doing here?"

"I know I've kept you away from your ocean lately. And this isn't right on it either, not like your condo, but it's close. I thought it might help center you before tomorrow. And . . ." Heat rushed to his cheeks, making him feel hot all over, the romantic sentiment on the tip of his tongue big. And telling. Not that he hadn't told Paris already about his history or how he felt about him, but this seemed different. More. Like putting it all on the line—his heart, his hopes, his forever.

"And what?" Paris said, as he rounded the front of the car and cozied up to his side, hand on his chest.

Mac covered it with his, sliding his fingers between

Paris's. "And this is where I fell in love with you. I wanted to spend tonight with you here. Make love to you here." In their own little oasis, away from the rest of the world that was horribly fast and dangerous these days.

Paris shoved him against the side of the car and stole a hard, deep kiss that had Mac seriously considering whether to skip the next surprise of the evening and go straight to the finale, right here against the side of the car. But then Paris drew back, his brown eyes staring up at him. "You're a good man too," he said. "More than you give yourself credit for."

"I hope you continue to think that."

"Oh!" He drummed his fingers on Mac's chest. "You have more surprises for me, don't you?" As fast as he'd spun getting out of the car, he did so again, darting for the cabin door. Only to find it locked.

"Oh!" Mac parroted back. "You need a key, don't you?" He took his time, unloading their bag from the trunk and strolling to the door.

"Now you're just being mean," Paris said with an adorable pout. Which disappeared as soon as he walked through the door into the candlelit cabin. He stood in the center of the space, wide-eyed and rotating to take it all in: the wildflowers on every surface, the spread of cheeses, nuts, and fruits on the table, the jazz music playing softly in the background. "Who did all this?" he asked. "The rest of the cabins were dark when we drove in, and all the witches' cars were gone."

"They've moved on." As the covens did, never too long in one place. "Mom and Dad helped out, with Rena and the kids"—he pointed at the cake under the glass dome on the counter—"pitching in too." He dropped the duffel at the end of the bed, then wandered back to where Paris stood in a stunned daze. Wrapping his arms around him from behind, he pulled him against his chest and nuzzled the crook of his neck, swaying them to the music. "I wanted us to finish that dance that got interrupted."

Paris rested his head on Mac's shoulder, giving him more access to his throat, more skin to pepper with kisses. "And where would it have ended?"

"Right here," Mac said, holding him tight. "Where you're the center of my world."

"And you mine." Paris angled his head, and Mac didn't hesitate to claim his lips, to sweep his tongue into his mouth and taste every bit of sweetness and light Paris had brought into his life, every ounce of love and desire Mac had avoided for so long but couldn't get enough of now.

Especially with Paris twisting in his arms and grinding up against him, his cock hard against the length of Mac's. "Is there any food that won't keep?"

Mac nipped at his lips, along his jaw, the lobe of his ear. "I just need to put the cheese in the fridge," he said, loving the tremors that quaked through Paris, the short breaths panted against the side of his face.

But not for long, Paris drawing out of his arms and holding up a hand when Mac started to reach for him, not willing to let him go. "Do that," he said. "Get a fire going, and I'll meet you back at the bed. I need to get my wits about me or this will be over way too fast."

Mac chuckled as Paris practically ran to the bathroom. He enjoyed turning Paris on, liked having him on the pleasure ropes for a change. He wondered if he could do more of that this evening, if he could try what he'd thought about that day Paris had been waiting for him with the toy. Mac hadn't packed the plug, but he bet Paris would still enjoy the stimulation. Mac sure would, the thought alone—of Paris writhing under his teasing tongue—getting him harder. When he stood from in front of the hearth, there was no hiding his erection. But then Paris wasn't hiding his either, standing naked beside the bed.

"Fuck," Mac cursed as he crossed the room. "Do you have any idea how beautiful you are?" The blush that rosied his pale cheeks only added to the devastating picture. "If I had any artistic talent at all, I'd paint these eyes," he said as he cupped Paris's cheek and swiped a thumb under the molten brown. He trailed his hand down, fingers barely touching skin, lifting goose bumps. "I'd paint these collarbones too, and the dip of your throat." He leaned forward, tonguing the divot, as he continued to travel south first with his hand, then his lips, kissing a path in its wake. "This valley that cuts between your pecs and your ribs and your abs." He sank to his knees and circled Paris's length with his fist, giving it a long, slow stroke. "This cock."

Paris let his head fall back on a groan. "You do okay with words. And the touch. Fuck, I love to be touched like this. So soft." Mac continued to stroke his cock, in no hurry, while he teased Paris everywhere around it with the soft kisses he seemed to love so much—his pelvis, his thighs, his sac—until Paris begged for more.

"You want me to kiss you here?" Mac teased, dropping one on the sticky head of his cock. He caught a bead of precome with his tongue and spread it around the head, pulling off after a flick to the underside.

Paris righted his gaze and his pupils were blown so wide that only a thin ring of brown remained, the dark black reflecting the violet of Mac's own eyes. "I want you to suck me off," Paris said as he plowed a hand into his hair, possessively clenching his fingers and urging Mac forward. "Make me come."

He swallowed Paris as far as his throat would allow, until he gagged, then did it over and over again, sucking and licking, teasing the tip each time he came close to drawing off, before plunging back down, using his hand to lengthen the strokes, especially as Paris increased the pace of his thrusting hips, putting more speed and power behind the movement, fucking Mac's mouth with abandon.

It was a sight to behold, the most beautiful man Mac had ever seen panting above him, at the mercy of his mouth, trusting Mac enough to let it all go with him. It was the biggest fucking turn-on, and Mac had to spread his own knees wider, had to make room for his own aching cock inside his trousers.

Paris's needy "I'm gonna come" didn't help his situation.

Mac grunted around his cock, and that was all it took, Paris coming in his mouth, filling it with come faster than he could swallow, some of it leaking out the corners of his mouth, because he would be damned if he didn't milk every last ounce of pleasure from Paris. When he was finally, completely spent, Mac drew off his cock with a parting kiss and stood.

"You made a mess," Paris said, sounding almost drunk as he wiped the come from Mac's chin. "And I'm not sure how much longer I can stand on these orgasm-jellied legs."

"Let's go, then," Mac said, his voice rough as he shuffled them the rest of the way to the bed, the two of them side by side on the edge.

Paris rested his chin on his shoulder and slid a hand over his thigh, sliding it higher until he was cupping him through his slacks. "We need to get this inside me."

Mac rocked up into his hand, the friction tempting, but his earlier thought still lingered, a fantasy he wanted to live. He rotated his face toward Paris's, whispering against his lips. "I want to taste you there first."

"Fuck," Paris cursed on a long, tortured groan. "You're gonna make me come again."

"Would that be a problem?"

Paris kissed the upturned corner of his mouth. "I love that smirk. I don't know if I want to paint it or your smile."

"Not the raven?" Mac asked as Paris began undressing him, his shirt the first piece of clothing to go.

"I thought about that too. I want you to see all the colors in your feathers. Like they are in your aura."

"What's it look like right now?" He lifted his hips so Paris could push his pants and boxers off, freeing his cock.

"Rivers of pink and red in a sea of flowing blue, violet, and green." He trailed a hand back up his leg, inside his thigh, cradling his balls. "It's beautiful, Mac. It's the peace you're supposed to have, that you deserve." Then fisted his cock, mimicking the long, slow strokes Mac had given him.

"Need you, Paris."

"You still want—"

"Yes," Mac said, wanting it more than ever, wanting all of Paris.

He waited for Paris to arrange himself on his stomach, his ass lifted by a pillow under his hips, then crawled between his spread legs, hands sliding up the backs of his thighs and palming his ass. Paris rolled his hips. "You gonna make me fuck this pillow?"

Mac answered by pulling his cheeks apart, exposing his hole, and lashing across it with his tongue.

Paris curled his hands in the sheets. "Again."

Mac was more than happy to oblige, happy to feast, happy to learn he was right—that his tongue teasing Paris's rim, dipping inside his hole, drove them both wild. Mac rutted against the mattress while Paris lolled his head with his groans, grabbed more of the sheets with each flick of Mac's tongue, and fucked the pillow with as much abandon as he'd fucked his mouth. And when Mac pushed one, then a second finger into him, opening him wider, getting him ready, he rode those with abandon too.

Trust and love, desire and hope pulsing along their bond the entire time.

A third finger and Paris cried mercy, thank fuck. "Get inside me, please."

"I've got you," he said, drawing those soft words over Paris's back again with one hand, while with the other he lined his cock up at Paris's hole and pushed inside him. They sighed in relief together, Mac stretching the rest of the way over him, lips against Paris's nape. "I could stay here forever."

"That's fine with me," Paris said, then thrust his hips. "Less so my cock."

Mac chuckled, Paris's torso under his rumbling with laughter too, until he started to move and their amusement became a series of grunts and moans, pleas for harder and faster.

As his orgasm approached, Mac stretched out his arms, hands seeking Paris's, his fingers sliding into the spaces between his spread ones. A perfect fit. Like their bodies, like their souls, which would get what they deserve. They'd get a choice, and Mac knew his. "I choose you, Paris. Forever."

Paris turned his head, his brown eyes swirling with love and a violet hue. "And I choose you. Forever."

He rested their foreheads together, lips brushing. "I love you. My soul is yours."

"And mine yours," Paris said on a gasp, body quaking and clenching around his. "I love you too."

"What we deserve," Mac promised as he rode the wave of pleasure with forever in his arms.

THIRTY-THREE

THE ONE THING HIS PARENTS, Rena, and the kids forgot to stock the cabin with was more tea. Not surprising, given their family was a coffee one, Paris the odd-tea-drinker-out. And not surprising that Mac had caved when Paris had rolled over in bed, stuck out that adorable bottom lip, and, arm slung across the rest of his pretty face, claimed dramatically that he would never be able to get out of bed without his leaf water. Mac had considered saying no just to keep him there in bed, looking like the beautifully debauched lover he was—his brown hair rumpled, his pale skin marked from lips and teeth, his morning wood tenting the sheet over his hips—but they had *a day* ahead of them, one in which Paris would carry the heavy mantle for their team and for Nature. Grabbing him the morning beverage of his choice was the least Mac could do.

He'd paused, however, over the threshold, fear creeping up his spine at leaving Paris out here alone, no witches in the other cabins, only a half arsenal of corvids in the trees, their numbers having been needed elsewhere overnight.

But then Paris had reminded him that no one except Kai had found them in the woods before, and the only reason he had was because Paris had told him exactly where to look.

"Ten minutes down to the motel and back," he'd pleaded with another pout. "I'll be fine."

Mac had relented, and thankfully, the little store had the olallieberry tea he favored.

"Anything else?" the clerk asked.

"I'm go—" he started to say, then noticed the collection of mugs behind her, one that made him think of Paris and grin. "Actually, can I get that yellow mug that says *Not Paint Water*?" The words were in black brush strokes, big and bold, on a can't miss background.

The clerk laughed as she rose on her tiptoes to reach it. "Painter in your life?"

"Yes," Mac said, smiling wider. "And he steals all the mugs for rinse buckets."

"My husband too," she said as she wrapped the ceramic mug in craft paper. "I ordered a half dozen of these and kept three for us."

"Did they work?"

She smiled, an amused, commiserative thing, as she handed him his bag of purchases. "Not one bit. Let me know how it goes with your man."

"Will do," Mac said, as he exited the shop for the car. He figured they probably would be back here, and that it would probably go about the same with Paris as it had with the store clerk's husband. And Mac wouldn't give a damn if it did, wouldn't care one bit if Paris filled any place they lived with paint mugs, as long as Paris was in his li—

The sudden, hard yank on the soul bond dropped him

to his knees, the mug shattering beneath his hand on the concrete, his heart and mind racing to decipher the fear and fire—the betrayal—coursing along the bond.

The resignation.

Mac yanked back. To no response.

Fuck.

He shifted, soaring into the air, and as soon as he did, he saw the smoke billowing through the treetops of the forest. He sailed across the highway and up the hill, cutting a direct path, slicing through the trees, the heat ratcheting up the farther into the woods he flew, the closer he got to the cabin.

A wall of smoke met him at the last dense arch of foliage where the other corvids had retreated. Sailing past them and under the arch, fire and flames greeted him on the other side, stinging his eyes and singeing the ends of his wings as he sailed around the burning cabin, searching for any signs of Paris.

Then hurtling back as a blast of heat erupted from inside the cabin, shattering the glass windows, buckling the walls, and caving in the roof, the entire structure collapsing.

He wasn't in there, Mac told himself. He couldn't have been. He would've gotten out, and the corvids would've escorted him to safety, to him, except they hadn't. They'd fallen back instead. Like they'd been ordered.

He dove closer to the ground, to where the front step of the cabin once existed. And that was when he saw it, in the morning damp earth, beside the massive footprint that could only belong to a giant.

A familiar oval-shaped paw print.

———

Mac shifted into human form a few feet shy of the villa's front door where Liam waited, trench in hand. "I felt you coming." His brother handed him the coat, and by his pinched brows and anxious gaze, Liam had also sensed the anger and desperation warring inside him. "What's wrong?" he asked. "Where's Paris?"

Mac shoved his arms into the sleeves and belted the coat around his waist. "Robin's in the barrel room?"

Liam nodded. "With some of the others. Where's Paris?" he asked again, voice pitched higher with worry for his friend.

Mac was sure his "Gone" didn't help, but he needed to get to Robin before the coyote was gone too. As it was, he was shocked the traitor had the gall to return here, unless he wanted to be caught. Which seemed to be the case, his golden gaze locking with Mac's as soon as he cleared the bottom step. "I can explain."

Mac flew at him, shoving him two-handed against the nearest wall and snarling through clenched teeth. "What did you do?"

"What he would have."

"Mac," Adam said, his footsteps approaching beside him. "What's going on?"

"I went out this morning to get Paris some tea, and this asshole led the giant right to him."

"How do you know it was the giant?" Liam asked.

Mac splayed a hand over his chest where the soul bond should be. "Because I felt it, here. Paris's fear and the fire he associated with him, the resignation when he surrendered himself." He pressed harder with the other hand against Robin still. "The betrayal. I found your paw print next to the giant's in the dirt outside the burning cabin. Why'd you do it? Why'd you betray us?"

Robin didn't put up a fight, didn't even try to skirt out of the hold Mac had on him. He could have—Robin was bigger, more powerful—but he gave him an explanation instead, their gazes locked. "I was patrolling last night. I found Brett on the outskirts of the property. Paris was right; he was the giant who attacked him. And he was coming after Pati. I offered him a different target."

"You brought him to our doorstep."

"He was ready, Mac. You're ready."

"He's on my fucking list, Robin." One more hard shove and Mac stepped back, desperation eclipsing anger, his voice ragged as he confessed the secret he'd shared with only a few. "I was supposed to deliver his soul that night at the altar in YB. Same as I had to deliver the first person I ever loved, and now you might've just doomed me to do it again."

Startled sounds echoed around the room, while in front of Mac, Robin paled and slumped against the wall. "I'm sorry," he said. "I didn't know."

"What else did Brett offer you?" Mary asked from where she stood at the head of the table. "Information on Atlas?"

Robin lowered his chin, running a hand across the back of his neck, a guilty tell Mac had seen countless times over the years, and anger surged once more. But not as fast and fiery as Jason's, the phoenix's glowing red fist connecting with Robin's nose. He reared back for another, but Kai backed him off at the last second.

Only for Icarus to take Jason's place, seething in Robin's face. "This vendetta of yours is going to get all of us killed. Do you get that?"

Robin wiped his bloody nose on his sleeve. "I get it, okay."

"Do you, Robin?" Adam said, as he pulled his partner back. "Because your actions say otherwise, time and again. How many more good people have to die for your selfishness? How many more souls can your conscious bear?"

It was a blow that even Mac, despite his own fury at Robin, felt in his gut, empathy not something he could just turn off.

Robin's guilty gaze shifted past Adam to him. "I'm sorry," he said, and Mac believed some part of him meant it. But another part of him also knew he'd make the same choice again, evidenced by his words. "But we know who the giant is now, and we know he'll be in one of two places tomorrow."

"What if I'm at the wrong one?" Mac said, letting the anguish he felt creep into his voice, the last hour of adrenaline burning out of him, leaving only fear and the very real prospect of despair. "What if I'm not there to save him again?"

"The Canyon Lands," Adam said, shifting into tactical mode. "We don't control and couldn't cleanse that one. There'll be more lingering souls to offer to Chaos."

"Or trust Paris to sell the Stick," Icarus said. "I'm angry as fuck at the dog, but he's not wrong about Paris being ready."

"We'll cover both," Mary said as she joined their group. She laid a hand on Mac's shoulder, her warmth pushing back at the threatening cold again. "Paris will show you, and when he does, we'll be ready."

THIRTY-FOUR

JUST AS MAC had put a hand over Paris's gut and asked him to make a call two days ago, Mac had done the same today, trusting his gut—and Icarus's logic—that Paris would convince Brett to bring him to the altar at the Stick for tonight's sacrifice.

And even though they'd felt certain that Brett would wait until tonight, until Samhain when the veil would be at its thinnest, they'd quickly moved into position yesterday, ready in case Brett accelerated the schedule. Mac had flown back and forth between the two sites yesterday, Liam on his wing, but tonight, he'd committed to the Stick. And like Mary had said, if it turned out the sacrifice was at the other altar in the Canyon Lands, Adam's team there would fight until Mac and the rest of his team made it to them.

Paris hadn't confirmed one way or another yet, hadn't shown him anything via their bond, which still hummed oh so quietly between them, almost as if Paris was hiding it. Not like at the condo, behind a wall of magic and inaccessible to Mac, but like he didn't want someone else to notice it. Mac took the comfort for what it was—Paris was still alive and the bond was still there when they needed it.

"We've got activity in the parking lot," Icarus radioed from where he was stationed with Jenn and members of the pack for the ground assault. Close enough to be inside the bank of fog that blocked the rest of them from seeing anything, but far enough out not to trigger anyone else's notice. "Group of cars are trickling in."

"Any sign of Paris or Brett?" Mac asked.

"Negative," Jenn reported, then after a moment added, "Visitors aren't human."

"Shifters or warlocks?" Jason asked, the lap of water audible against the side of the boat where he, Kai, Mary, and several of Paris's recruits waited. Two warlocks for the field and another to stay behind and protect Mary.

"Bit of both."

"Witnesses," Liam said from beside Mac on the bluff where they were stationed with the flock. "Like at the other sites."

They'd been prepared for that. No reason to think tonight—especially tonight—would be any different.

"Fucking hell," Icarus cursed.

"What?" Mac snapped, harsher than intended, but his nerves were already fraying after twenty-four hours of waiting with no indication of when or if he'd ever see Paris again.

"Atlas just got out of one of the cars," Icarus relayed. "And he's back in his villain attire. Fully suited."

No *if*, then, just *when*.

"What the fuck is he playing at?" Jason growled, and from Mac's vantage on the bluff, he saw the light of a fireball through the fog, on the water near where their boat should be.

"Call the other team down," Mary said. "This is the site."

Mac clasped his collar, ready to yank his shirt off and shift, but Liam stopped him, hand around his biceps. "Not yet, brother. I know you want to fly, but we can't go until Paris is there."

"He's right," Jenn said. "We can't risk scaring them off. We might never find Paris, then."

He appreciated that Paris was her primary concern, not the giant, but fuck, this was killing him. And he was lashing out at any target. "Then someone tell Jason to put the fucking fireball out," he gritted between clenched teeth. "I can see it from here."

The light on the water vanished, the Bay dark again.

"What's going on?" Mac asked after another minute passed.

"The witnesses are gathering," Jenn replied. "In a semi-circle like at the ridge."

"Atlas is behind the altar," Icarus added as the wind gusted around them. "That fucker, what is he doing?"

"Babe!" Mary chided before Mac could. "Details."

"It looks like he's sucking power from the other warlocks. He's got his hands raised. Why's his magic yellow? It's usually green. Fuck, he's chanting something, but I can't hear it."

"It sounds like Gaelic, Mac," Jenn said.

Kai gasped. "Is he trying to open the portal himself?"

"No," Mary said. "But he's thinning it out more." Belying her typically confident voice was an undercurrent of very real fear. Mac had only heard her sound like that once before, that day in Portola when she'd faced down Vincent, ironically under Atlas's arm. "I can feel it."

And in the next instant, Mac felt something too.

Paris.

A single pulse—agony—pushed down the bond, and then the earth groaned, as if torn apart by some awful magic, and a blast of light that Mac could see through the fog lit the Stick.

"He's here," Jenn confirmed. "With Paris."

That was all the go-ahead Mac needed, and this time, Liam didn't stop him, taking to wing beside him, the flock at their backs as they streaked toward the site.

Comm no longer in ear, Mac couldn't hear whether Jenn and Icarus were leading the pack members into the fight, nor whether Jason and Kai were powering the boat of magical reinforcements to shore, but he had to trust his team. Trust that Adam's contingent would get here too as fast as magic and motors would carry them.

He and Liam sliced through the fog, and when they emerged on the other side, the battle was already in full swing. Jenn and other members of the pack in their big coyote bodies, tumbling with other shifters. Icarus and Jason and their warlocks engaged in combat with several other warlocks. Kai in the air, a white beacon surveying the scene, causing others to look up and gasp, giving their own fighters a chance at the upper hand.

But as Mac scanned past the battle to the altar, he wobbled in flight, the sight of Paris in pain rocking Mac to his core. Blood poured from fresh cuts on his arms and legs and his back bowed and hands fisted as souls poured through him. The scene had been gruesome the first time around, but now that was the man Mac loved on the altar, his forever being tortured, and Mac felt every ounce of his pain in his own soul.

KRAA! Liam screeched beside him and, wing under his, kept him aloft as the initial shock—the agony—ripped through him.

Then morphed into anger, into single-minded purpose.

He called back his thanks, and Paris's head on the altar lolled their direction, his eyes wide and glowing violet, tracking his and Liam's flight toward him, before they squeezed shut again and his back bowed once more, his mouth forming the same words, over and over.

Help me.

What horrible deaths was he reliving behind those eyes each time a soul traveled through him? How many could he bear before his own weakened body gave out? Before his soul joined them and the bond between him and Mac was severed? They didn't have time to waste.

Mac pushed love and strength, pride and reassurance along the bond, everything he couldn't say in raven form, then, with his brother at his side and his flock at his back, dove for the giant.

And streaked back when fireballs and magic sliced through their wave of black, searing the tips of his wings. He banked left, taking half the flock with him, Liam going right with the rest, and they spread wide, too many targets for one warlock and one giant, the rest of the witnesses otherwise occupied.

And more of Mac's forces arriving by the second, Robin's big rusty-blond body tearing onto the scene, Abigail's feline form on his heels, and Adam with his guns at the ready. More of the pack and Paris's recruits charging in and overwhelming the witnesses.

The giant hurled his fireballs, growing more distracted and disoriented by the second as souls that passed through Paris escaped to the water, toward where Nature called them away from Chaos. Atlas spun, as if sensing her there, and Robin pounced, taking a fireball hit to his pointed ear yet still sailing across the altar at the warlock and taking him down. He opened his jaws on a roar . . . and then nothing but yellow mist, Atlas snapping away from the scene.

Mac called to Kai, pointedly directing him back to the boat, to Mary in case Atlas reappeared there and sending half the flock with him. He kept the remaining corvids with him and Liam, circling the giant, the heat rolling off him in waves, no doubt scorching Paris where he lay in front of him. They needed to neutralize him before he disappeared into another fireball and charred everything, including Paris.

Mac circled back over Adam, Liam gliding to his flank, in position for them to build on their experience with the ridge giant. And Robin was already where they needed him.

"Robin!" Adam shouted, as if reading Mac's mind. "Grab him!"

The coyote reared up and snapped at the shreds of the giant's clothing, using it to pull him back, exposing his chest for Adam's silver bullets, then clamping hold of his shoulder and dragging him back further, heedless of the heat and flames. The smell of burnt fur tickled Mac's senses as he and Liam swarmed with their brethren around the giant's head, pecking and flapping their wings, drawing his fire and fists their direction and away from those on the ground below.

"Brock!" Icarus called. "Chains, now!"

The warlock they'd recruited spread his glowing blue hands, a heavy silver chain appearing out of thin air between them. Adam grabbed one end, Icarus the other, the two humans who could handle it running around the altar, then splitting off in opposite directions, circling the giant's waist. Brett howled and flailed, shaking off Robin, but Adam and Icarus, the pack at their backs, the flock harassing the giant from the front, dragged him back, back, back over the rocks and to the water's edge.

Where Mary waited, hanging off the side of the boat, her hands in the water, ripples of green cresting and crashing, circling Brett's ankles as Adam and Icarus hauled him in.

Turning him back into nothing but a small power-hungry, hate-filled man.

The silver chain dissolved, and before Brett could make a run for it, before he could transform back into the giant, Robin crashed into the waves and held his body under, the assassin doing what he did best, Nature his witness to the kill.

"Mac!" Jason yelled from behind them, and Mac wheeled in the air back toward the altar where Jason was hauling Paris down with Brock's help. "Mac! We're losing him!"

THIRTY-FIVE

MAC LANDED ON HIS FEET, in a dead sprint, chanting "No, no, no . . ." as he slid onto his knees beside Jason. He hauled Paris into his arms, holding his body close. He was too cold, too still. The bond between them pulsed erratically, dimming bit by bit.

"Come on, Paris, stay with me." He cupped his cheek, wiping away the tear tracks that stained his beautiful, pale face. He forced more love, more gratitude, more pride through the bond. "You did it, baby. You slayed the giant. Now come back to me. Open your eyes, *please*."

"Mac," he mumbled weakly.

"I'm right here."

His eyelids fluttered open, and hazy violet irises stared back at Mac. "Help me."

"What do you need?"

"The stars. Mom."

Mac lifted his gaze and cursed the fog.

"The ocean," Paris rasped.

"We're right by it."

"Can't hear," Paris said, shaking his head, eyes slipping closed again. "Need to, one last time."

Mac's heart stopped, then caved in on itself. "No, no, no, we said forever."

"Please," Paris whispered on a shallow breath.

Beside them, Liam kneeled and clasped Mac's shoulder. "Do you need me to help?"

He glanced at his brother, finding his face as wet as Mac's felt, his eyes swirling with shared grief.

Mac nodded, and Liam helped him to his feet, steadied him as he adjusted Paris in his arms. He turned toward the water and met Adam's stormy gaze. Asked him, without a word, if he was ready to fulfill a promise.

Adam nodded.

And with that reassurance, Mac put one foot in front of the other, Liam on one side, Jason on the other, as he carried his precious cargo across the slippery rocks to the water's edge where Mary waited.

He sank to his knees, letting it wash around them, and the smile that graced Paris's face was pure peace, the same one he wore in sleep and ecstasy, in everyday life as he brightened the world around him, the same one that had convinced Mac to love again.

Mary kneeled beside him. "Are you ready to let him go?"

"Never."

"Are you ready to take his place?"

Caught off guard by her question, Mac looked up and found Mary's gaze on Liam.

"I am," his brother answered.

"What—" Mac started, then gasped as the water around them turned green and violet, and the souls he'd seen escape came rushing back across the top of the gentle break-ers, back to Paris, as if he and Mary had called them. They surrounded Paris in his arms, warming his body and caging in his soul, keeping him there.

With him.

"You've done enough," Mary said. "Both of you. Now they want to return the favor, and so do I."

A spark of hope caught, like the embers of the fireplace back at the cabin. "We can have forever?"

"You can have what you deserve," she said. "Liam is the reaper now. You'll deliver no more souls until it's time to deliver his," she said with a nod to Paris. "And you'll deliver yours with him. Many, many years in the future, if you can help it."

Mac laughed, improbably, then leaned over and pressed his forehead to Paris's warming one. "Do you still want forever with me?"

"Forever," Paris whispered back, sealing the future Mac hadn't dared hope for until the man in his arms grabbed hold of his soul and refused to let go.

PART THREE

MAC & PARIS

THIRTY-SIX

"THESE THREE MISSING persons cases came into the office after the Rift anniversary." Mac handed Liam copies of his department files, then nodded at the two green-hued crime scene paintings leaned against the wall of his study. "Paris was able to call two of the souls to him. Got us some more details."

Since the Stick, Paris wasn't only able to dive into souls' memories. He was also able to call souls to him, a game changer when it came to Mac's cold cases and the department's missing persons ones. It had barely been a week since the Stick, and they'd already solved multiple cases. Mac wanted him to slow down, to pace himself as he recovered, but Paris was determined to help, to make sure as many souls as possible reached their destination before winter solstice, not wanting anyone else to try and manipulate them for evil.

Liam flipped open the first file and glanced between the photo of the young woman in the file and Paris's painting of that same woman floating in a lake, a letterman jacket thrown over her. "She's on my list," Liam said, then set that file aside and opened the next. "Not on my list," he said of the second person Paris had painted, "but I'll send out word to the other reapers." He snapped a photo of the painting.

"And we'll keep investigating the third," Mac said.

Liam dropped the files on the desk, then rested back against the edge. "This doesn't seem so bad."

Mac sighed and leaned a hip next to his, raking a hand through his hair. "I should have let all of you help me sooner."

"It was a good lesson for me." He bumped their shoulders together. "And you're a good mentor too, regardless."

"He's also a good husband," Paris called from the adjoining room. "So far!"

Liam laughed out loud, one of the things Mac had always loved about his brother. Something he was trying to learn to do more of himself, smiling as he joked, "I think Mom left that tent up on purpose."

"I don't think there's any *think* about it." Liam pushed off the desk, chuckling. "You and Paris will be down for dinner tonight?"

"Are you sure you don't want to move up here?" Mac asked as he followed him into the other room. "This is the reaper's perch, and you're the reaper now."

"The big house is our home. This is yours and Paris's."

"Until we get a place by the ocean," Paris amended from behind his easel at the window. "Tell Rena I'll bring bread."

"We'll see you in a bit," Liam said with a departing wink before disappearing out the door.

"Did you have another vision?" Mac asked as he circled the couch. "Or are you painting your oce—" The rest of his question died, words caught in his throat, blocked by his heart that had suddenly lodged there. "Paris . . ." He stared in awe at the painting of himself, asleep on his stomach in their bed, a soft smile on his face, his left hand on the pillow, wedding band bright, reflecting all the colors of the aura that shimmered around him. The blue, violet, and green flowing, the rivers of red and pink a beautiful swirling design throughout. "This is what it looks like?"

"Now, yes," Paris said, as much awe in his voice as Mac felt in his soul, in the bond that sang between them.

He reached out a hand, drawn to the swirls of red and pink, but Paris stopped him short, grabbing his wrist. "It's still wet."

Using Paris's hand around his wrist, Mac turned him in his arms, his front to Paris's back, admiring the painting over his shoulder. "You went with the smile?"

Paris angled his head to look up at him, his big brown eyes warm with love and a touch of violet, their soul bond shining through. "I've got forever to paint the smirk."

"I like the sound of that," Mac said as he brushed his lips across his husband's, repeating the promise that tied their souls together until their end, as Mary said, hopefully many, many years in the future. Until then . . . "Forever."

THIRTY-SEVEN

PARIS AND PAIN were officially broken up.

His wounds were healed, his soul intact, his bond with Mac stronger than ever, singing whenever he paused to listen to it, all the chords of his favorite jazz tune the background music of a life—a forever—he couldn't have imagined a month ago. Aside from missing his ocean when he wasn't at the condo in YB, he was happy here under the Talahalusi sun, soaking up its warmth and inspiration. Free from his own painful past, committed to freeing from pain the others who'd suffered under his father, and working with Mac and Liam to free souls from the pain that kept them lingering here on this plane.

Which was what brought him here today, Mary at his side. "This is where it happened?" he asked.

She kneeled and put a hand to the earth, digging her fingers into the ground and mixing up the layers of clay, silt, and ash. A clearing in the forest, ten years after a devastating magical fire. A myriad of colors he'd have to paint when he got back home, once he helped the lingering soul here find his way.

Mary stood and saplings sprouted in the divots she left in the ground. She brushed the dirt off on her jeans and nodded. "This is it."

As if the coyote shifter sitting on the ground, back leaned against a charred mess of wood at the edge of the clearing, didn't give it away. "What are you doing here?" Robin rumbled as they approached.

He looked like hell, his golden eyes dull, his rusty-blond hair matted and overlong, his right ear scarred, the days-old dust on his sunken cheeks crisscrossed with dried tear tracks.

Paris lowered to the ground in front of him, sitting with his legs crossed, then offered Mary a hand down as well. "Do you actually stay with the pack, or are you out here every night?" she asked Robin.

"What difference does it make?"

"Because none of us should exist alone," Paris said. "Especially not someone whose aura is as wrecked as yours. And I thought Mac's when I met him was bad." He whistled low, and the coyote cracked a smirk.

"You sound like him."

"Mac?"

"Icarus."

Paris shrugged, taking it as a compliment to be compared to his sassy friend. "Maybe we're both just people who will give it to you honest."

"And what are you here to give me honest, medium?"

"For starters, forgiveness."

He snarled. "I don't need—"

"Bullshit," Paris snarled right back. "You do, and I give

it to you, because you were right. We were ready; I was ready." There'd been a time when Robin had made him doubt himself, but when it had mattered most, he'd believed in him. "And now the giants are gone."

His golden gaze drifted over Paris's shoulder, the direction he and Mary had come, back toward Monte Corvo. "Do they forgive me?"

"No, and they won't for a while."

"And you're no closer to finding Atlas, are you?" Mary asked.

"What's it matter to you? You gonna 'fess up finally?"

When she didn't reply, Paris reached out and laid a hand on Robin's knee, drawing the coyote's attention back to him. "That's the other thing I'm here to give you."

His eyes grew wide. "Atlas?"

"No. The truth about the day your sister died, *if* you want it."

Robin's gulp was audible in the otherwise quiet clearing, only the buzz of late harvest bees zipping from one plot to the next breaking the silence. Until eventually Robin stuttered out a shaky "Yes."

Paris closed his eyes and felt for the souls connected to the tragedy that had occurred here ten years ago. He could call Deborah or David across the plane, anyone else who'd been here that day, but where he could help it, he didn't disrupt souls from their final resting place. And besides, he'd sensed another lingering soul here, other than Robin's living one, as soon as they'd neared the clearing—a shifter who'd been pressed into service for the other side, who'd known something they'd waited all this time to share.

Contact made, the vision shifted, Paris in his shoes on the edge of a green-tinged battle in the same clearing, only there were more trees then and a wooden structure where Robin sat.

Deborah and David were easy to spot among the other combatants, she the largest coyote on the field, he a human with orange and red magic rippling across his skin. On one knee, he was desperate to save his family but struggling to keep the phoenix in check.

A bolt of yellow magic zipped their direction, and Paris swung his gaze in the direction it had come. A suited Atlas stood wielding globes of magic, sending one after another Deborah and David's direction. Until someone grabbed his arm, sending a bolt off-kilter. Paris followed its trajectory, afraid it was the one that killed Deborah, but it missed, just barely, and he turned his attention back to Atlas.

And gasped. There were two of them. The suited one from before and another one in a kilt and leather gauntlets. Side by side, Paris noticed the differences he'd missed the other night on the altar when he'd been consumed by pain and betrayal. The suited one's blond hair a shade darker, his green eyes shot through with yellow, a mole at the corner of his right eye that Paris knew Atlas didn't have.

"Don't do this," the kilted Atlas argued. "I can't bring you back from this."

"First, it was Canton. Now, it's you. Is Cole here too?"

"Listen to me."

"No," the stranger barked, because that was who he was to Paris—a stranger, not Atlas. "I'm done listening. I'm done falling in line. I'm done pretending we're not as powerful as we are."

"Chaos will use you."

"You'd know," the stranger sneered. "It's my turn now."

Yellow and gray swirled in his eyes, blotting out the green, and he conjured two sizzling yellow globes of magic.

And Paris knew with heartbreaking certainty what came next.

"Evan, no!" Atlas shouted, but he was too late.

With one hand, Evan flung a globe at him. Atlas barely managed a magical green shield before getting slammed back into a tree, his magic no match for Evan's, which disappeared Atlas from the scene before he could throw the green globe he'd had in hand.

Before Evan, with his other hand, hurled the other yellow globe directly at Deborah.

Paris ripped himself out of the vision, nearly losing his stomach as he gasped for breath, his own fingers digging into the earth, reconnecting to this plane, waiting for the ringing in his ears to give way to the jazz notes of the bond that anchored him here. He'd come back with Liam for the lingering soul, give him the peace he deserved, but Paris had needed to get out of there, to plant his soul firmly back here before it got sucked further into tragedy and pain.

"It wasn't him, was it?" Mary asked once he finally righted himself with Robin's help. At some point during his vision, the coyote had moved to his side, a steadying hand wrapped around his biceps.

"It wasn't," Paris said, and Robin yanked back his hand like he'd been burned. "What do you mean it wasn't him?"

"It wasn't him," he repeated. "He's after the same thing you are. The person who killed your sister. Evan."

Mary gasped.

"You didn't know?" Robin said.

"Not all of it." Sadness flashed across her hazel eyes before she shoved to her feet. "Well, we're going to find him first." She kicked Robin in the knee with her booted foot. "Let's go. We have a new mission."

"We?" Robin rose, almost as quickly as his bushy blond brows. "They'll think I took you."

"They already think you're a traitor. What's one more betrayal?"

As Paris rose, he worried how many more barbs like that Robin could take. Yes, he was a selfish ass, but beneath that front was a man ravaged by guilt, by a heart that was too big for the tragedies that continued to pummel it, by the death he doled out for a living. Darkness soaked his aura, and Paris feared he'd never escape it, that no one would ever be able to crack through his walls and find the heart that had so much to offer. So much potential for joy and good.

For love.

If he'd just believe he deserved it. Paris stepped closer and lifted a hand, cupping his dusty cheek. "They may not trust you, but I do. I see your aura. I know what haunts you, why you need to fix this. And on behalf of all of them, I'm trusting you with her."

A flicker of light in his golden eyes. "He was lucky to find you."

"I'm the lucky one," Paris said with a smile, remembering Mac's soft sleepy one as he'd left that morning. The same one he got to wake up to for the rest of their lives. Anyone with a heart as big as Robin's deserved that kind of happiness too. "We both got what we deserved. And you will too."

———

For all the latest updates on new projects, sneak peeks, and more, sign up for Layla's Newsletter and join the Layla's Lushes Reader Group on Facebook.

———

Reviews are an invaluable tool when it comes to spreading the word about great reads. Please consider leaving an honest review for *Paris and the Reaper* on your favorite review site.

Thank you for reading!

ACKNOWLEDGMENTS

First, a big thank you to everyone who waited patiently for this book. I really did intend to get it out sooner and then life conspired to delay things. But good news, I'm already at work on *Atlas* so despite what the preorder date says, you will get it sooner! Because OMG, I loved writing in this world again. Mac and Paris came so easily, and Robin and Atlas are already super chatty. I can't wait to bring you the final part of the *Soul to Find* story.

As for Mac and Paris's story, my sincere appreciation to:

Kim for all the whispers that kept these characters talking and me writing. Your love for these two assholes—and your tireless PA efforts to take care of everything else while I listened to them—helped make this a swift, relatively pain-free write.

Annabeth and Hailey for all the word sprints and cheers. This book was all gas, no breaks, and you gamely sped along with me.

Allison and Erin for always being there with encouragement and distraction when needed. And if you want more reapers, go read Allison's *Only Mostly Dead*.

Kristi, Adam, and Lori for your editing and proofing wisdom.

The Grey's Promo team and Kelly for the promotional support.

And last but far from least, Kelley York of Sleepy Fox

Studio, who created the stunning cover for this book and the entire *Soul to Find* series. This cover was actually the first one, a premade I snatched up because it was so gorgeous and moody and featured a raven. As someone who grew up with a grandfather who rehabilitated injured crows, who as a kid had many a JoJo as "pets," who fed a whole family of them during the pandemic and who now has a family in the woods behind her, this cover is so very special to me.

As is this book. I hope you all find it special too. Thank you for reading!

ALSO BY LAYLA REYNE

For the most up-to-date list of titles and a helpful reading order, please visit www.laylareyne.com.

Soul to Find:

Icarus and the Devil

Jason and the Storm

Paris and the Reaper

Atlas and the Traitor

Agents Irish and Whiskey:

Single Malt

Cask Strength

Barrel Proof

Tequila Sunrise

Blended Whiskey

Angel's Share

Fog City:

Prince of Killers

King Slayer

A New Empire

Queen's Ransom

Silent Knight

Perfect Play:

Dead Draw

Bad Bishop

King Hunt

Best Play

Standalone Stories:

What We May Be

Under the Table

Table for Two:

The Last Drop

Blue Plate Special

Over a Barrel

Changing Lanes:

Relay

Medley

Freestyle

ABOUT THE AUTHOR

Layla Reyne is the author of *What We May Be* and the *Agents Irish and Whiskey, Fog City*, and *Perfect Play* series. She writes sexy, intense LGBTQIA+ romance featuring competent adults in kitchens, sports arenas, car chases, and other high-stakes situations. Whether it's adrenaline-fueled suspense, rival athletes, vampires and shifters in alt-realms, or love mixed with mouth-watering foodie goodness, queer folks finding happily-ever-afters is guaranteed.

You can find Layla at laylareyne.com, in her reader group on Facebook—Layla's Lushes, and at the following sites:

BB bookbub.com / authors / layla-reyne

f facebook.com / laylareyne

instagram.com / laylareyne

tiktok.com / @laylareyne